PICKING UP THE PIECES

A CLOVERLEAF NOVEL

JESSICA PRINCE

Copyright © 2018 by Jessica Prince
www.authorjessicaprince.com
All rights reserved.
No part of this book may be reproduced in any form or by any electronic or mechanical means, including information storage and retrieval systems, without written permission from the author, except for the use of brief quotations in a book review.
First edition: July 2013
Latest edition: February 2018

DISCOVER OTHER BOOKS BY JESSICA

SECOND HOPE SERIES
The Little Things

Tangled Up With You

ASHLAND SERIES
Dead to Rights

WHITECAP SERIES
Crossing the Line

My Perfect Enemy

Turn of the Tides

THE PEMBROOKE SERIES:
Sweet Sunshine

Coming Full Circle

A Broken Soul

Should Have Been Me

WHISKEY DOLLS SERIES
Bombshell

Knockout

Stunner

Seductress

Temptress

Vamp

HOPE VALLEY SERIES:

Out of My League

Come Back Home Again

The Best of Me

Wrong Side of the Tracks

Stay With Me

Out of the Darkness

The Second Time Around

Waiting for Forever

Love to Hate You

Playing for Keeps

When You Least Expect It

Never for Him

REDEMPTION SERIES

Bad Alibi

Crazy Beautiful

Bittersweet

Guilty Pleasure

Wallflower

Blurred Line

Slow Burn

Favorite Mistake

Sweet Spot

THE CLOVERLEAF SERIES

Picking up the Pieces

Rising from the Ashes

Pushing the Boundaries

Worth the Wait

THE COLORS NOVELS

Scattered Colors

Shrinking Violet

Love Hate Relationship

Wildflower

THE LOCKLAINE BOYS

Fire & Ice

Opposites Attract

Almost Perfect

CIVIL CORRUPTION SERIES

Corrupt

Defile

Consume

Ravage

GIRL TALK SERIES:

Seducing Lola

Tempting Sophia

Enticing Daphne

Charming Fiona

STANDALONE TITLES:

One Knight Stand

Chance Encounters

Nightmares from Within

DEADLY LOVE SERIES:

Destructive

Addictive

To Josh and Jacob,
Thank you for making my life whole.

PROLOGUE
EMERSON

PAST

"What the hell do you mean, you enlisted?" I couldn't catch my breath. It felt like the ground had just been pulled out from under me. My best friend, the person I had grown up next to my entire life, just informed me that he had enlisted in the Marine Corps. This couldn't be happening.

"Emmy, baby, it's okay," Luke told me in a conciliatory tone. "It's just the Marines. It's not the end of the world."

I didn't understand how he could be so casual when I was completely petrified.

"Are you out of your *freaking mind*?" I screeched. "We're in the middle of a war, Lucas! You just signed up to go over to a war-ravaged country and potentially lose your life in the process. Please explain to me how that isn't the end of the world?"

If anything were to ever happen to Luke, it would be the end of *my* world. I had no doubt about that. The pain in my chest was so acute, it was as if someone had reached inside and was squeezing my heart.

Luke grabbed my shoulders and pulled me into his chest.

Wrapping my arms around his waist, I inhaled his familiar scent and let it calm my frayed nerves. Luke had always done that for me. He'd always been my peaceful place when things got too rough. I couldn't imagine what my life would be like with him not in it. I couldn't bear the thought.

"Baby girl, I know you're mad right now, but this is something I just have to do," he said as he ran his hand down the back of my head. I knew he needed my blessing to feel good about his decision, but this was the first time in my life I had trouble giving it to him. I wanted to be selfish and scream at him that he couldn't do this... that I couldn't support him. But I didn't. I knew this meant a lot, and I wouldn't take that away from him.

"Why, Luke?" I needed to understand. I pulled my head away from his chest and looked up into his eyes. I could see the memories that haunted him running through those emerald pools, and knew exactly what he was feeling before he even said anything.

Letting out a deep sigh, he responded, "I just do." Dropping his arms from around me, he ran his hands through his black hair, sending it into a disarray that would have looked messy on anyone else, but always managed to look sexy on him. "I can't stay here any longer. You just graduated and will be leaving for college soon. What's left for me after you're gone?" I knew my leaving was weighing on him, but I honestly had no clue that he was taking it *that* hard. Luke and I grew up living next to each other in our small town. He and his parents moved in three houses away from me when he was six, and even though he was two years older than me, we'd instantly become friends and had been inseparable ever since.

The two of us had been through more than any person our age should ever have to go through, and we both managed to get through it with the help of each other. It was my window he would climb through when he had to sneak out of his house at night to get away from his parents' screams as they fought with each other. It was me who would bandage up his cuts and wipe away the blood when his dad drank too much and took his anger out on Luke. I hated his father with a passion and had no respect for his mother. She allowed Luke to be abused all those years and did nothing to stop him.

He was the shoulder I cried on for months when I lost both of my parents in a car accident when I was only thirteen. My parents were the complete opposite of Luke's. For all the bad his folks did, my mother and father tried to counter with acts of kindness. They took Luke under their wing without question, easily accepting him as my best friend. I adored them both with my whole heart, and when they passed they took pieces of me with them that I knew I'd never get back.

Even though my grandmother moved into our house to help raise me, it was Luke that I went to whenever I felt like life was a weight too heavy for me to carry on my own. I could always count on him to help lift my burdens.

So while the idea of him not being a car ride or a phone call away felt like a knife in my gut, I understood. I knew that the only reason he hadn't left his drunk of a mother was because I was still there, three houses away. Now that I was going to be four hours away attending college, I understood that Luke viewed this as his chance to get out of our little town and finally make something of himself. Unfortunately, that didn't make my heart hurt any less. His leaving was going to hurt almost as much as losing my parents. That was how close we were. The only consolation I had was that he'd at least come back to me.

"I understand," I finally conceded, even though I didn't want to. "But I swear to God, Lucas Matthew Allen, if you get dead I'll do whatever voodoo necessary to bring you back and *kick your ass.*"

His deep chuckle rumbled through me as he pulled me back

into his strong arms for another hug. "No worries, Emerson Kristine Grace. I promise you, I won't get dead."

"I'm gonna hold you to that, you know." I smiled up at him for the first time since we started our conversation. Just looking into his eyes made me feel a little lighter, took away some of the anxiety I was feeling.

But not all of it.

"I'd expect nothing else, baby girl."

CHAPTER ONE

EMERSON

IT HAD BEEN a week since Luke dropped the bomb that he'd joined the Marines, and it was only a few days until he left to start basic training. I'd been counting down each hour and trying not to throw up at the thought of him getting hurt. I was with my friend Savannah, trying to keep my mind off of all things Luke and military related, which was proving to be much harder than I thought. I was supposed to be helping her pack up her closet and throw out all the junk she wouldn't need to bring to our dorm room when we left for college. But instead, I found myself lying back with my head hanging off her bed, staring into space and getting a massive blood rush to my brain.

"You know, if I'd known you were just going to lay on your fat ass and not help pack, I would've asked Jeremy to help me. At least he's nicer to look at." She stuck her tongue out at me and threw a balled-up pair of socks at my head.

I laughed and threw them back at her, hitting her right between the eyes. "First of all," I replied, sitting up to look at my friend, "my ass isn't fat. It's J. Lo-esque." She let out a snort at my comment even though she knew I was right. I had an awesome booty. "Secondly, I am *so* much better looking than

Jeremy." Savannah and her boyfriend Jeremy had been an item since freshman year of high school. To say their relationship had been tumultuous was an understatement. The two of them fought more than anyone I'd ever met, but when things were good between them, it was like no one else in the world existed. Things were good at the moment, but that could change quicker than Savannah switched out shoes. And she had *a lot* of shoes.

"This is true," she said with a snicker. "But at least Jeremy puts out. You're just a tease."

"Touché," I replied, then fell back to her bed and stared up at her ceiling again. I was trying my hardest to pull myself out of the funk Luke's leaving was creating, but it was just so damn hard.

"Seriously, Emmy, get the hell up and help me pack, or I'm not gonna be your roommate."

I let out an annoyed groan as I dragged myself off her bed. "Fine. But I don't want to hear you bitching if some of your shoes just happen to disappear. You don't need this many pairs anyway." I reached into Savannah's closet, pulled out my favorite pair of black and white Converse, and proceeded to stuff them into my purse. She just rolled her eyes at me and kept packing. I loved Savannah, and the two of us had been close since the second grade, but the chick had a serious shoe hoarding problem. Not that I was one to complain since I got to reap the benefits of her little obsession and all.

"So when's Luke heading out?" I could hear the concern in my friend's voice. She knew how difficult the thought of being away from Luke was for me. Savannah was my best girlfriend, and she completely understood the bond that Luke and I shared.

"Day after tomorrow," I mumbled. Just thinking about it depressed me and brought back that deep ache in my chest.

"It'll all work out, Emmy, you'll see. What with modern

technology and all, you guys will be able to communicate at the click of a button. It's not like you'll be using carrier pigeons or smoke signals."

Letting out a laugh, I threw a strappy platform wedge at her head. "Smartass." I appreciated her trying to cheer me up a little by being Suzy Brightside, and I tried to act the part, but I knew I wasn't pulling it off as well as I'd hoped.

"I know this is tough, but the two of you can email and write letters. Trust me. It'll be like he's right there." She looked back at me with a genuine smile, making me feel slightly better. One of Savannah's gifts was making a positive out of most negative situations. When she wasn't able to do that, it always helped that she was funny as hell. You couldn't help but laugh when you were around her.

"You're right. I know."

"And you're going to see him tonight, huh?"

"Yep. He's taking me out for one last dinner before he heads out." I was anxious about this dinner. Part of me was excited to be spending one of his last nights here with him, but it was also bittersweet. I looked down at my watch and saw it was a quarter to five. Luke was picking me up at six so I needed to start getting ready. "Speaking of... I should probably book it. Gotta get gussied up." I blew her a kiss and waved my fingers at her.

Savannah looked around her room at the mess we had made and threw her hands in the air. We had managed to pull the entire contents of her closet out onto her bedroom floor. Not a single thing was in a bag or a box. I really hadn't succeeded in helping her at all.

"Gotta go," I said as I raced to her door.

"I hate you, you know," she yelled after me.

"Love you too, Savvy!"

LUKE HAD TAKEN me to the only nice restaurant in town. It was fancier than my grandmother's diner but not too fancy that jeans and a nice shirt wouldn't do. We spent the entire time talking and laughing. We reminisced about our childhood and our friends. It was one of the best nights I'd had with Luke, and as I lay in bed replaying the whole evening over and over, I couldn't help but feel the weight of his impending departure resting on my chest like a ton of bricks, making it impossible to breathe.

We'd just spent our last night together in who knows how long. I felt like such a horrible friend for having to fake my happiness for Luke when it came to his decision to leave. He'd always supported everything I did, and until now, I'd always supported him. I was a terrible friend and the guilt settled in my gut like week-old pizza.

Rolling over onto my side, the depression started to take over like a never-ending black void. My thoughts had occasionally drifted into rather morose territory since my parents' death, and whenever I got in one of those moods Luke and Savvy were the only two people who could pull me out. Knowing that I was about to lose one of them was like losing a limb. The phantom pain remained even after the appendage was long gone.

The dark thoughts had started to settle in when I suddenly heard the sound of my window being lifted. When I glanced in the direction of the noise, I could easily make out the perfect outline of a body that I knew from years of experience could only be Luke's. My mind rewound, trying to recall the last time Luke snuck through my window, but it had been so long I couldn't remember.

Luke's father bailed on him and his mother soon after he turned sixteen, and even though his mother never stopped drinking, the physical abuse and Luke's need to escape his home life had disappeared with his father. I had missed those nights we spent together, but I was thankful that the person who made Luke's life hell was gone, and couldn't hurt him anymore.

I held my breath as the covers were lifted and the bed shifted under Luke's weight. I finally released it when his arm slide around my waist and pulled me into the solid wall of his chest. Chest to back, we laid there for what seemed like hours. Neither of us saying a word, both content to just *be*. Out of everything I was going to miss about Luke, his warmth would be what I missed the most. Laying silently, I let the tears flow, knowing they were inevitable, and I was helpless to hold them back. I'd managed to keep them at bay so far, but this was just too much.

"Baby girl, please don't cry," Luke whispered into my hair, pulling me tighter to him as his breathing turned harsh.

I sucked in a breath and tried to speak around the lump in my throat. "I-I'm sorry," I stuttered. "I'm not trying to upset you, I swear." I twisted in his arms so we were face to face. "I just didn't think I'd be this sad," I said, giving a weak smile, trying to make light of my tear-streaked face as I looked into those fathomless green eyes. He just stared back at me, not saying a word as he ghosted his fingers across my cheek and down my neck. He'd touched me a million times in the span of our friendship, but for some reason this seemed different. There was an intimacy in this touch that I'd never felt from him before, and it caused my heart to stall before starting up again at a faster pace.

I felt him take a deep breath as he tucked a loose strand of hair behind my ear. "I know, Emmy." He spoke so softly I could barely hear.

"I feel like I'm losing a part of me, Luke. I'm going to miss you so much."

His breath shuddered as if he was trying to hold back his own tears. "I'm going to miss you too, baby girl. More than you know. But you aren't losing me. You'll never lose me. I promise."

That did it. His promise cracked something inside me, and there was no holding back from what I did next. My entire body was swamped with emotion that I had no chance of controlling. Wrapping my arms around his neck, I pulled Luke's face closer to mine and pressed my lips to his. It wasn't my first kiss, but considering it was the first one with Luke it felt more meaningful than any of the kisses that had come before. Fear and hope fluttered deep down in my belly as I memorized the curves of his plumps lips with my own.

I couldn't lie and say I'd never pictured kissing Luke before, he was one of the most gorgeous guys I knew. I just never had the guts to pursue something other than friendship. But with him leaving, I felt a desperation I'd never experienced. The risk of damaging our friendship disappeared. A nagging voice in the back of my head told me that if I didn't show him how I really felt at that very moment, I might never get the chance again.

I *had* to kiss him. I had to know what being with him would feel like. There was no telling how long it would be before I saw him again, and I would hate myself if I didn't at least try.

Luke's entire body froze against mine for just a moment, but when I ran my tongue over his bottom lip his mouth opened and returned the kiss with more intensity than I had started it with. I rolled onto my back and pulled his strong, hard frame on top of mine in a silent plea. Breaking the kiss, Luke looked down into my eyes cautiously, as if he was trying to get answers without asking the questions. Afraid of him pulling away, I wrapped him in my limbs and held tight. "Please, Luke," I whispered. The need I suddenly had for him was so much greater than anything I had ever felt before.

"Emmy, we can't. You've never..." When he trailed off it became clear he was struggling to do the right thing. I could see the war waging in his beautiful eyes, but I was determined. "Emmy, honey, you deserve so much better than me. Your first time should be with somebody you love."

The words poured past my lips before I had a chance to stop them. "I *do* love you, Luke. I always have." I'd never intended to say that, but once it was out there, it just felt right. I knew to my very soul that this was supposed to happen. I wanted him more than I wanted my next breath.

Luke's massive frame was like stone as he hovered above me. If I was going to get him to realize that we were meant for each other, I knew I had to make the leap first. And just pray he followed after me. "Please, Luke. I need you." I reached a point where I didn't care if I sounded desperate. Everything I was saying was completely true. I needed him more than I had ever needed anything. I was desperate for him.

Those were the last words either of us spoke to each other. We let our bodies communicate everything else that needed to be said. Hours later when the sun began to rise and peak through my bedroom window, I started to drift to sleep with a sense of contentment that had settled into my bones. My body was deliciously sore. Remembering how Luke treated me like the most precious thing he'd ever come into contact with created a deep blush that spread all over my well-loved skin. It was pure bliss.

What I didn't know then was that the happiness wouldn't last. The next day Luke would tear my heart to shreds before he disappeared from my life for good, leaving nothing but pain and devastation in his wake.

Unaware that my future was about to be stripped away, and I would be left in tatters I fell into a dreamless sleep with a smile on my face.

CHAPTER TWO

EMERSON

PRESENT DAY

"DOLL FACE, I SAID ORDER UP!" Lenny yelled from the pass-through between the kitchen and the front of the diner. It was the middle of the dinner rush and I'd already been working since six that morning. To say my patience was wearing thin was a serious miscalculation, since I'd already run totally out of the shit hours ago. I was three seconds away from murdering my line cook.

"Lenny, if you call me doll face one more time, I'm gonna plant my size seven so far up your ass you'll be sucking my toes in reverse." The diners snickered as I laid into him but I didn't find it in me to care. I'd run all out of 'professional' sometime around lunch. My body was now running on copious amounts of caffeine and pure bitch. Not a combination you wanted to mess with.

"Sounds kinky," I heard Savannah say as she breezed through the door of my diner and parked her butt on a barstool like she owned the place. "I gotta see you pull that one off,

Emmy."

I snapped my dishtowel at her as I grabbed the order from Lenny's window and shoved it at her. "Make yourself useful, Savvy. Help me wait some of these tables."

She stared down at her manicured fingers like the idea of waitressing offended her. "Don't you have waitresses for that kind of thing?"

"I do," I responded shortly, about to turn my wrath from Lenny on to her. I was already at the end of my rapidly-fraying rope. "But Tiffany called in sick. Half of my waite staff are out with the flu and I'm in the middle of a dinner rush. So, please, be a good friend and wait some damn tables!" The last part of that sentence didn't come out as a request at all, and she knew it. Savannah was amazing at reading my moods (not that my current one wasn't obvious). She might poke the bear a time or two just for fun, but she knew not to mess with me when I was in bitch mode.

"All right, all right. Don't get your panties in a twist, darlin', I'll help. But I'm not waiting on Old Lady Murphy. She's a shyster and I expect good tips if I'm gonna be doing manual labor." She might occasionally annoy the ever-living crap out of me, but I could always count on Savannah when I needed her.

"She's not a shyster, Savvy. She's on a fixed income."

Savannah hopped off the barstool and headed around the counter to grab an apron. "Fixed income or not, the old bat could at least tip ten percent on a seven dollar meal. I've got a mind to spit in her coffee."

I chucked a scone at her head and pointed my index finger. "Do that and I. Will. End. You," I hissed between clenched teeth.

Giving me a little chuckle, Savvy held her hands up in surrender. "Okay. Easy tiger, no sneezers for Old Lady Murphy." She walked away from me and quickly started waiting tables. She complained about it every time I asked for help, but I was convinced she secretly loved it. She was a flirt with all the male customers and a gossip with the women. The people in our town adored my best friend, even when she was prickly.

The rest of the evening progressed at the same steady pace as it always did. That was one of the good things about living in a small town like Cloverleaf, Texas; you could always count on consistency.

Friends that Savannah and I had throughout school came in for good gossip and even better food. Mr. Clements from the hardware store stopped by for some of the homemade pie that made the diner so famous. The Robertson family came in for their weekly blue-cheese bacon burgers. It was business as usual. Virgie May's had been a staple of our town for as long as I could remember. My grandmother opened up shop back in the fifties, and the diner had been going strong ever since.

When I took over ownership four years ago, it had never been my intention to stay on for the long haul. But things changed and life dealt me a blow I wasn't expecting. I had to pull up my big girl panties and accept the inevitable. I'd never be a lawyer or a doctor. It seemed I was destined to forever be a diner owner. The only thing I'd ever cure was hunger, and I was okay with that. *Now*. It took me a long time to get to that feeling of contentment, but once I did I was able to breathe a little easier.

"You feel like heading over to Colt's for a few beers and some pool?" Savannah asked as she wiped down the counter at the end of the night. I had just flipped the sign to *Closed* and locked the front door. The only thing I wanted to do was go home to my cute little house and soak in a nice, hot bubble bath. Heading over to Colt 45, the town's local bar, was the furthest thing from my mind.

"Savvy, if it requires me keeping this bra on, I'm gonna have to pass. I have a standing date with my bath tub and a bottle of wine."

She rolled her eyes at me, already knowing this would be my answer. "Ditching the bra might help in getting you more drinks," she teased with a wag of her eyebrows. "You sure you don't want a chance to take some more of Brett and Jeremy's money?"

"While the idea of wiping the floor with the guys in pool is appealing, the answer is still no."

"Fine, worth a shot." We headed out the back door into the parking lot, and I silently thanked God that my day was over. I was beyond exhausted. "You hear that Sherriff Carlson brought on a new deputy?" Savannah asked as we made our way through the dimly lit gravel lot.

This was the first I was hearing of Cloverleaf getting a new deputy. In a town so little, change wasn't exactly commonplace, and new people moving in was about as exciting for us as Friday night high school football. Whoever this new deputy was, the town was sure to be buzzing about him for weeks to come. I was a little surprised it hadn't been mentioned to me before now. "Nope. Any clue who this guy is?"

Spinning her keys around her finger, Savvy answered. "No clue, but I'm hoping he's a hotty. This town needs some new eye candy."

Ever since she and Jeremy called it quits for good years back, Savannah had made it her goal in life to be a serial dater. She didn't exactly sleep around, but she wasn't above accepting an invitation for an expensive dinner every now and then. "Only because you've worked your way through every eligible bachelor in all the closest counties," I replied with a smirk.

"Hey," she chirped in mock defense. "A girl's gotta have her fun somehow."

I leaned against my beat up Honda Civic and pulled off my shoes, wiggling my toes to get the blood circulating back to them. I breathed a pained sigh for my poor, abused feet before responding. "You know, you could have just married Jeremy."

Savannah let out a huff of laughter. "*Please.* We were a toxic combination. The only reason we stayed together as long as we did was because the sex was rockin', and he had a *huge—*"

"*Enough!*" I squeaked before she could finish, all but plugging my ears with my fingers and shouting *la la la la la* to keep from hearing what she had to say. "Jeremy's like a brother to me. The last thing I need is to know how big his shlong is." There wasn't enough brain bleach on the planet to get that imagery out of my head.

Her grin was positively wicked. "I was going to say bank account, gutter brain." That was so *not* what she was going to say.

"Mmh hmm," I hummed suspiciously. "Sure you were."

"Besides, we're better as friends anyway."

I reached behind me and unhooked my bra, sliding the straps off beneath the sleeves of my t-shirt and pulling it out the bottom. "Says you. That boy's still hopelessly in love with you."

"He'll get over it," she replied flatly, all humor having fled her tone and expression. Jeremy was a sore topic for Savannah. She loved him, but for some reason it just hadn't been enough. They tried to make their relationship work, but sometimes loving someone doesn't mean they're who you're supposed to end up with. I hurt for both of them. Watching two people who cared so much about one another, but couldn't make a relationship work no matter how hard they tried was bad enough. Both of those people being my best friends made it ten times worse.

"Anyway..." I knew she was attempting to close down that particular subject matter, so I let it slide. I didn't want to make her uncomfortable no matter how badly I wished she would confide in me about Jeremy. "I'll let you get to that bath and wine before you get completely naked out here in the parking lot. Love you, doll face."

"Smartass."

Shooting me a smirk, and a little finger wave, she headed off to her brand new Lexus parked a few spots from my clunker, flipping her shiny blonde hair in her wake. Even though Savannah's education gave her more options than I had, she insisted on moving back to Cloverleaf after college in order to stay close to me. She claimed it was only because we were soul sisters and separating would be like removing the other woman's better half, and while I totally agreed that functioning together was much easier than it would be apart, I hated that she had given up so much for me.

It took a while to get over the guilt, but I held an immense amount of love for that girl for all she had done for me. I couldn't have asked for a better friend than I had in Savannah. I might have been an only child, but the minute I met Savannah I gained a sister for life.

After climbing into bed later that night, I laid there staring up at my ceiling, thinking about the direction my life had gone in. There had been so much bad, but I somehow managed to make it through to the other side relatively unscathed. I hadn't done it alone, not by a long shot, but it wasn't lost on me that the one person I thought would always hold my hand through all the bad was nowhere in sight.

My rock, the one person I'd always depended on, hadn't been there for me for the past eight years. Luke might have been the person to help me through some dark times growing up, but I'd managed to pull myself through some even darker ones without him.

I repeated the mantra I'd had in my head since the day he'd destroyed my heart so long ago. I didn't need Luke Allen. He meant nothing to me. He was just a boy I used to know.

Losing him hadn't been easy. In fact, it hurt like hell, but over time he'd become nothing more than a bitter memory.

I don't need Luke Allen, I chanted in my head as sleep started to pull me under. *He's nothing to me. He's just a boy I used to know.*

And with that, I drifted off to sleep.

I WAS in the middle of refilling Tracey McCreedy's coffee the next morning when Savannah came barreling through the front door of Virgie May's with Jeremy, Brett, Gavin and Gavin's girlfriend, Stacia, in tow. Stacia and Jeremy had been in the same grade in school as Savannah and me, while Brett and Gavin had been in Luke's. After Luke took off for parts unknown, we all remained tightknit. Including all those people, and a few others, I had a pretty awesome circle of friends that I was forever thankful for.

If it had been anyone else storming through the door, I might have been aware of the shift in the air of the diner, but Savannah's always had a flare for the dramatics.

"Emmy, we gotta talk," she said as she barged up to Tracey's table.

"In a sec, Savvy. Kind of in the middle of something here." I ignored her theatrics and continued to serve my customers.

"Seriously, Emerson. You need to come with me, right now." She only ever used my full name when she was about to rip me a new one, or had too much to drink, so hearing those three syllables from her lips caught my attention and caused goose bumps to spread over my skin.

"What is it?" Looking up at her, I noticed she was worrying her bottom lip between her teeth. Her eyes cut to Jeremy, who was busy looking at his shoes like he'd never seen work boots before. The rest of the gang refused to make eye contact, causing my anxiety to spike. "What's going on? You guys look like someone just set fire to the animal shelter, and you have to break the news that the puppies didn't make it out." My humor was lost on my friends, and the hair on the back of my neck stood straight up at their lack of reaction to my joke.

"Can you please just come with me?" Savannah grabbed my hand and started pulling me toward the kitchen. "Like right now. I need to talk to you in the kitchen. *Right. Now.*" Allowing Savannah to drag me toward the back, coffee pot still in hand, I started to really freak out. It had been a long time since I'd seen my friends this distressed. Something was really wrong. I just didn't know what.

Glancing around the diner, I noticed that we had the attention of all the customers. Some looked intrigued by the show unfolding in front of them, others had looks of pity on their faces.

What the hell is going on? I thought as the bell above the door chimed, alerting me of another customer. "Take a seat anywhere," I called, my eyes still on Savannah. "Someone will be with you in just a sec."

Suddenly, Savvy's face turned an unhealthy shade of white, and her eyes were the size of salad plates. I heard Gavin mumble curse words from behind me, and a soft "oh no" from Stacia. The five of them automatically closed ranks around me as I turned to look at the person who had just walked into my diner.

Then I heard it. And my blood ran cold.

"Hey there, baby girl."

CHAPTER THREE

EMERSON

HEY THERE, *baby girl.*

Those four words had haunted me for so many years.

This can't be happening. This can't be happening. I thought if I just kept repeating that in my head, I'd wake up from this horrible nightmare. It had to be a dream because there was no way in hell *he* could be standing right in front of me. God, or Karma, or whoever was in charge couldn't possibly be that cruel... Right?

My entire body had gone numb the instant I heard those words. All of the air had whooshed out of my lungs. I was frozen solid. That was, until I dropped the pot of coffee I'd been holding, causing it to break and splatter scalding coffee all over my legs, burning the shit out of myself in the process.

"Shitfucksonofabitch!" I hollered, dancing from foot to foot. I knew I looked like a complete idiot, but I couldn't help it. *That really freaking hurt.* Jeremy and Brett immediately jumped into action, grabbing paper towels from the counter and wiping down my legs. Tears pricked the backs of my eyes as I looked at the angry red welts now covering me from knee to ankle.

Fucking Texas weather! I thought. If it hadn't been a million degrees outside, with a thousand percent humidity, I could have worn jeans instead of shorts, and prevented second degree burns on my shins. But *noooo*. Texas weather sucked, which meant it was hotter than the devil's butthole outside. Hence the shorts and burned legs.

I was immediately pulled out of my weather-bashing trance when I felt Savannah's fingers gripping my forearm. "Holy shit. Are you okay? Did that hurt?" I couldn't process all of the emotions raging through me at that very moment. I felt anger, fear, anxiety, and a little bit of giddiness, which just pissed me the hell off.

"No, Savvy." I clipped out. "It felt fucking awesome... Of course it hurt!" I was being an absolute bitch to a person who didn't deserve it, but it was taking everything in me to keep from falling to my knees and bursting into tears, or scream my fury at the top of my lungs. I was a mess! Luke was standing right behind me. What the *hell* was *Luke* doing *standing right behind me?*

Spinning around, I narrowed my eyes at the culprit that caused the coffee pot massacre. It had been eight years since I'd last laid eyes on Lucas Allen, and in all those years he'd only managed to get even *more* attractive. Those deep emerald green eyes, surrounded by dark black lashes that would make any girl envious, burrowed right into my soul as he stared back at me. I might have been in meltdown mode, but it wasn't lost on me that all six feet four inches of him was looking dangerously hot in a tan deputy's uniform. So this was the new deputy that Sherriff Carlson had hired. *Perfect*.

"Shit, baby girl. You okay?" Luke came rushing over to me and hunkered down to inspect the welts that had already formed on my legs. The shock caused by his touch made me jump back. "Don't move, Emmy. Let me take a look."

Who the hell does this guy think he is? "Don't touch me," I whispered through clenched teeth.

"Emmy, please. Just let me take a look, okay? I've dealt with burns before. I know what I'm doing." As he reached for my leg again, it took every ounce of my energy to resist the urge to haul off and kick him square in the face.

"I said, *don't. Touch. Me.*" The heart-clenching pain that took me so long to get rid of was coming back in full force. I was struggling to breathe and control my tears all at the same time. I was fighting a losing battle to control my own body. And it was all *his* fault. I hated that one look at him had already undone years of work to repair my heart.

"Emmy—" he started, but was interrupted when Savannah pushed between us, all five feet three inches of her radiating so much anger she was practically vibrating. This was *not* going to be good.

"Look here, Special Officer Asshat. I don't give a shit if you're the goddamned Surgeon General himself. She said not to touch her, so you don't *touch her!*" Each word out of her mouth got louder and louder until she was yelling in his face. If I wasn't in the throes of a full-blown anxiety attack, I might have been impressed with Savannah's attempt to bow up to a guy that was over a foot taller and at least ninety pounds of solid muscle heavier.

Luke slowly rose to his full height and glowered down at my friend with sheer intensity. I had to hand it to her, she didn't even blink.

Grabbing her arm, Jeremy tried to intervene and calm Savannah down. "Easy there," he whispered into her ear, eyes locked on Luke the whole time, like he was preparing for whatever was to come. "Stand down, killer."

She spun around and leveled Jeremy with a death glare so intense, I fully expected him to burst into flames. *"Fuck that!"* she screeched. "He can't just walk in here after eight years and act like he didn't do a damn thing wrong!" She spun back around to face Luke again. "You call her baby girl one more time, and I'm going to punch you so hard, you'll be shitting teeth for a week! You don't get to call her that. You aren't even worthy of breathing her air."

The scene in front of me had escalated to epic proportions. I was finally able to suck in enough air to kick start my brain back into action. "*Enough!*" I yelled. "This is a public restaurant, not a goddamned boxing ring. We are *not* doing this here." I addressed Savannah first. "Honey, I know what you're doing and I love you to pieces for it, but I got this, okay? You can retract the claws." I jerked my attention over to Luke, wishing I had laser beams in my eyes. "You need to leave. Now."

"Emmy—" he started, but I cut him off.

"No! For eight years, I wasn't important enough to get so much as a letter from you. You don't get to roll back in to *my* town and show up at *my* diner acting like nothing happened. You haven't had a thing to say to me in eight years, and I don't have anything to say to you now. Get the hell out, Luke."

I turned my back on him, not bothering to watch him walk out the door and turned my attention to the patrons of Virgie May's. "And all of you," I addressed the crowd collectively. "Drink your damn coffee, and eat your damn breakfast. Don't act like this is the first time y'all have ever seen drama here. This is Cloverleaf, for Christ sake."

With that, I turned and headed to the office in the back of the diner. My little rant having just expended all my energy.

I had just collapsed into my office chair and begun to massage my temples when the door creaked open. I didn't open my eyes to see who it was until I heard something being placed on my desk. Looking up, I saw Brett pouring bourbon into two shot glasses. Once full, he slid one in front of me and took the other for himself. "Brett, it's eight thirty in the morning. Not really the time to be pulling out the hard stuff." I initially objected, mainly because that was how a respectable person would react to having hard liquor for breakfast. Truth was, I fully intended on getting wasted.

"After the shit that just went down, Emmy Lou... I'd say now's the perfect time." Brett was another one that I'd known for forever. Even though he'd always been closer to Luke when we were teens, he and I managed to form a tight bond after our so-called friend disappeared. I guess the mutual feeling of betrayal was a good catalyst. After all, I wasn't the only one that Luke left behind.

Picking up the shot glass, I downed the amber liquid in one gulp, reveling in the burn as it slid down my throat and settled in my belly. "Set up another," I said as I slid my glass back in front of him. He took his first shot at the same time I took my second.

We sat in amicable silence for what seemed like forever until Brett finally broke it with the one question I feared the most. "What are you going do, Emmy? It's a small town. Someone's bound to let it slip."

I knew what he was asking, but there was no way I would consider talking about it again. It had been so long ago and set my life on a path that I wasn't proud of. It had taken everything in me to pull myself out of the downward spiral that loss caused me. "Let them talk. It's not like I didn't try to get ahold of him, Brett. You know that. He's the one that refused to respond to any of my messages." I poured another shot and drank. I was starting to feel the effects of the bourbon. My heart rate had slowed and my shoulders were beginning to feel nice and relaxed. "I've finally got my shit together. I'm not going to let him come back and ruin everything I've worked for."

I could feel the burn of tears in the back of my throat trying to make their way out. I wasn't going to let that happen. I'd cried too many times over what Luke had done to me. I was done with that. He didn't deserve my tears. Seeing me struggle to keep my emotions in check, Brett stood and walked around the desk, wrapping me in his arms. "I know, Emmy Lou. I know. You're one tough bitch, that's for damn sure, and I've got your back no matter what."

I hugged him back as tight as I could. "I know, Brett. And I love you. But call me a bitch again and I'll stab you."

We both laughed and squeezed each other one more time before Brett pulled away and left the office. It wasn't long before I remembered the burns on my legs. The drama from earlier and the alcohol had helped me to forget they were there, but when I accidentally slammed my shin against the desk drawer I was quickly reminded. "*Motherfucker!*"

Savannah came breezing through the door with the first aid kit in her hand. "I figured you'd do something like that when Brett told me he'd given you booze." She opened up the kit, removing gauze and burn cream. "Up you go." Holding my legs by my ankles, she lifted them onto the desk and started applying the cream. "Soooo...." She dragged out. "You want to talk about it?"

"Nope," I replied dryly as I closed my eyes and laid my head back against the chair.

"Didn't figure you would, so I won't bother you." She was full of it. She had every intention of bothering me, and that was confirmed when she continued. "But I will say this. If Deputy Douche Nozzle steps foot into Virgie May's one more time, I'm gonna bust a cap right in his ass."

I let out a snort of laughter when I looked up at her. "Not that I don't appreciate the Ya-Ya Sisterhood solidarity and all, but you've got some crazy scary anger issues brewing right now, sister."

She let out a deep sigh, placed the cream back in the kit, and closed the lid. I could tell by the expression on her face that the jokes were over. It was Serious Savannah time. "Look, Emmy. I know that growing up Luke was always your best friend. But you were mine."

Crap, here come the tears again.

"It never upset me. I wasn't jealous or anything like that, I just want you to know. You aren't just my best friend, you're my sister, and when you hurt, I hurt."

There was no holding them back. Those stupid tears forced their way to the surface and started trickling down my face. "You're my sister too, Savvy. You're my family. You guys are all I've got."

Savannah started crying too. "So then you understand... when Luke left you the way he did, and you went through all that bullshit those first few years... Well...it killed me watching you falling deeper and deeper, and not knowing how to stop it. I can't watch you go through that again."

I stood and pulled Savannah into a tight embrace. "Oh, honey. That's not going to happen again, I promise."

She sniffled and we both pulled apart, wiping the tears from our eyes. "Good," she said with a little laugh. "Because this time, I'll kick your ass so hard you won't have a choice but to snap out of it."

This made me laugh too. "I love you so much, Savvy girl."

"Love you too, Emmy."

CHAPTER FOUR

LUKE

I KNEW my return to Cloverleaf wasn't going to be met with banners and fireworks, or a parade in my honor, but I'd still been ill prepared for just how hard it was actually going to be.

Emmy's hatred toward me wasn't surprising considering how I left things between us, but knowing that didn't stop the pain that slammed into my gut like a sledge hammer at the sight of the disgust resonating in her beautiful blue eyes.

I was a fucking idiot. I'd been so consumed with my fears about Emmy that I never stopped to think about the repercussions of abandoning the rest of my friends as well. It was evident that my decision to keep everyone at a distance in order to keep Emmy back wasn't my brightest idea. Obviously, our whole crew had banded together to back Emmy in her treat-Luke-like-the-asshole-he-is campaign, not that I blamed them. I *was* an asshole.

After the epic blowup between me, Emmy, and the notoriously bitchy Savannah, any hope I had that I could re-kindle those past relationships was flushed right down the shitter. When Emmy had so lovingly banished me from Virgie May's, I returned to my shit-hole apartment with my tail between my legs. What I needed was a good night's sleep and a few shots of whisky. Oh, and a plan... I needed a plan.

I woke the next morning feeling a little better about Operation Win My Friends Back. At least until I got to the auto body shop that Jeremy owned. When I'd returned to Cloverleaf a few days earlier, I'd been surprised to see that one of the only things to change in the past eight years was the Starbucks that now sat on the corner of Main and Pinehurst. Before Jeremy's garage, I'd stopped off there since I wasn't going to risk bodily harm by going back to the diner for a cup of coffee. I remembered that Jeremy always had a killer caffeine addiction, so I was hoping the big ass cup of solid black in my hand would be a good enough olive branch. But I didn't want to get my hopes up too high.

I walked into the bay where Jeremy was working on a black '67 GTO. I sucked in a fortifying breath and took my shot. "Hey man, that's a fine ride you got there." Jeremy just looked at me as he wiped his hands with an old oil rag, not saying a word. "Uh," I started, feeling more uncomfortable with every passing second. "I brought you a coffee." I extended my hand holding the Starbucks cup.

Quirking a brow, he reached out and took the drink. "Starbucks? Emmy'll kick my ass, she sees me drinking this." The smirk on his face told me that he'd love to see that happen.

I let out a short burst of laughter as I rubbed the back of my neck. "Figured Starbucks was a safer bet. I don't think it'd be too smart to go back to Virgie May's just yet."

That got a full blown shit-eating grin from Jeremy. "Maybe not ever, brother."

I couldn't help the disappointment that stirred in my gut at that thought. "I'm kind of getting that man." This definitely wasn't going like I'd hoped. Blowing a puff of air past my lips, I raised both hands in surrender. "I'm just here to say I'm sorry,

Jer. I've got a lot of apologizing to do, and I figured you'd be a good starting point."

"Well color me flattered, soldier boy, but if you don't mind, I got a lot of shit to do," Jeremy replied insolently. I'd never had a gift for words, and my obvious shortcoming was making this whole situation even harder. I'd fucked up. I had no one to blame but myself, but I had no idea how to go about making it right with the people I'd cared about my whole life.

He turned his back to me and continued working on his car. Taking that as an opportunity, I dug deep and said the only thing that had any chance of working. "I'm an asshole, Jeremy."

That got his attention fast. "Well, that's a better start, at least... Go on," he said, waving me on to continue.

I couldn't help but laugh. "Look, there isn't anything I can say that could possibly make up for the shit I did. I was in a fucked up place when I left, man." I paused to try and get my thoughts sorted before continuing. "I was a dick. I know that, but... everyone was moving on with their lives. Y'all were all going to make something of yourselves, and there I was, stuck in the same piece of shit house, at the same piece of shit job, day after day, nothing ever changing for me. I just couldn't do it anymore."

Jeremy threw the rag on the hood of the car and rested his hip against it, crossing his arms over his chest as he gave me a stormy look. "That doesn't explain you cutting off all contact with anyone that ever cared about you. No one gave a shit you joined the Corps. We were all proud of you for making something of yourself." He let out a heavy sigh and shook his head before going on. "It's the fact that when you left, you severed all ties with every one of us, Luke. That's the shit that's hard to let go of."

He was absolutely right. And the truth was, I didn't have a single good excuse. "I know, Jer. I know. And if you decide to hate me forever, I'll understand. It's just... after the shit I did to Emmy..." A ball of pain swelled up in my throat. Emmy. *My* Emmy. *Christ*, I'd messed up so damn much. The hatred that flared in her gaze the day before was the most painful thing I'd ever experienced.

Swallowing down the lump, I continued, "I couldn't even stand to look at myself in the mirror. How the hell was I supposed to face any of you when I already hated myself more than any of y'all possibly could?"

If I'd wondered whether or not Emmy told any of our friends about our night together before I left I'd gotten my answer the second I walked into that diner. The animosity that had poured off of them in waves wasn't only because I bailed. It was so much more than that.

"I fucked everything up that night, and instead of trying to make it right, I took the coward's way out. It's a shit reason but I need you to know, if I could go back and do things differently, I would. There isn't a day that's gone by that I don't regret everything I did."

Jeremy tilted his head slightly to the side as he studied me. "I'm not gonna lie to you, brother. That shit you pulled with Emmy was royally fucked up. You got no clue how bad that hurt her."

Hearing that things had been hard for Emmy after I left burned like acid in my stomach. The thought that I caused her any pain at all killed. I could deal with her contempt, but the thought of her in pain was almost too much to bear. "I know. But I'll tell you now, I'm going to do everything in my power to make things right."

"That's all I ask, Luke." Jeremy reached his hand out to shake mine, and I knew we'd made some headway in getting things back to how they once were.

"So, we cool?" I asked, extending my hand to his.

"Getting there. I might hold you over the flames a few more times, but we'll get there."

My head fell back on a burst of laughter. It was the first real laugh I'd had in years. It started off foreign and awkward, but ended up feeling damn good. "I'll take that, brother."

Having the serious part of our conversation over and done with, Jeremy went back to work on the GTO, shifting the conversation to something else. "So, you talk with your Ma?"

That was just another thing on a long list of shit I wasn't looking forward to dealing with now that I was back. "Not yet," I replied, ever the coward.

"You're going to have to deal with that sooner or later."

I ran my hands through my hair. It felt weird after eight years of having a military buzz cut to actually be able to run my hands through it, but Emmy always talked about how much she loved my hair. She said the inky black strands were softer than anything she'd ever felt, and that she could spend the whole day running her hands through my hair and never get bored. Remembering that, I grew it out before I came back. I needed every advantage I could get with that girl.

"Believe me," I finally replied, "I'm hoping for later."

Eyes to the engine, Jeremy spoke sagely, "Sitting on shit like that just makes it fester."

"When did you get so wise?" I asked with a chuckle.

His attention shifted to me, a smirk on his face. "What are you talking about? I've always been wise. You forget that over the past eight years?"

I shifted uncomfortably at the mention of my long absence. I wasn't sure I'd ever get used to that being thrown in my face. "Guess I did."

"Tell you what, I was just about to head out to lunch. Why don't we hit up the deli on Main? You know, since you're banned from Virgie May's and all."

"You're a fucking riot, man," I deadpanned, punching him in the arm.

We started walking out of the bay toward the street. "So what do you think I should do to get back in Emmy's good graces?" I wasn't going to tiptoe around the real reason I was back in Cloverleaf. I left behind the one and only girl I ever cared about, and I was determined to get her back.

The air around us suddenly shifted, and I noticed Jeremy's demeanor had changed from casual to serious in a matter of one sentence. "Honestly, I don't know, Luke. Some shit went down after you left. It's not my story to tell, and I won't break her confidence, so don't even ask. But I really don't know what to tell you. All I know is if she's going to forgive you, it's going to take *a lot* of damn work on your part."

Jeremy's cryptic message didn't sit right with me, but if there was one thing I knew about him it was that he was loyal to his core. If Emmy had a secret, there was no getting it out of him, no matter how hard I pushed. It didn't matter though. He said it would take a lot of work and I was more than prepared to put in the man hours.

"Come on, dude," Jeremy called back to me. "I'm starving and you're buying. I figure if you really want to make things right, I got at least a year's worth of free meals coming my way."

One down, way too many to count to go.

At least I was off to an okay start.

CHAPTER FIVE

EMERSON

"I CAN'T *BELIEVE* THAT TRAITOR!"

Savannah was on a roll. We'd just left the salon after some much needed mani-pedi time to see Jeremy and Luke walking out of the deli across the street, laughing. *Laughing!* I guess that meant Jeremy had forgiven the asshole. I refused to admit it out loud, but seeing my buddy laughing with Luke "The Dickhead" Allen stung... like *a lot*. But with him back in town, I'd made the decision to be the bigger person. Even if it killed me... which it very well might.

"I've got a mind to rip both of them a new one," she continued. I just let her rant. Trying to stop Savannah when she was on a tangent was like trying to stop a train by standing on the tracks with your hand out... dangerous and extremely stupid. "That's it! I'm so silent treatment-ing his ass."

I blew out a frustrated breath. "Isn't silent treatment typically used for a guy you're *in a relationship* with? Last I checked you keep turning him down."

She waved my statement off like it was nothing. "It'll work, trust me. Jeremy can't stand it when I don't talk to him. He depends on his daily dose of the awesomeness that is me, and now he's not going to get it," she harrumphed.

I rolled my eyes skyward. "Oh yeah. You're sure showing him."

"Bet your sweet ass I am."

I stopped in the middle of the sidewalk and looked at my best friend. Time to do that whole bigger person thing. *God this sucks.* "Look, while I'd love nothing more than to watch Luke die a slow, agonizing death, preferably while I stood over him kicking the hell out of his junk, that's just not going to happen. He's back, and there's nothing you or I can do about it." I raised my hand to stop her oncoming argument. "He lived here for a long time and he had a lot of friends. If those guys decide they want to forgive him for bailing, then that's their decision." Feeling pretty good about my speech so far, I sucked in a breath and finished it off. "I might not be able to forgive and forget, but I'm a big enough person not to hold it against someone else who can."

Look at me... all noble and shit!

Savannah stared at me in disbelief for several seconds before declaring... very loudly, "That's such *bullshit!*"

Huh, well that wasn't the reaction I was expecting.

"Don't think I don't know what you're doing, Emerson Grace. You can pull that bigger person crap with someone else. I know better. You want to kick Jeremy in the sac just as bad as I do!"

Grabbing her by the arm, I dragged her around the corner. The last thing I needed was for everyone else to know I was full of it because of Savannah's big mouth. "Okay, okay," I admitted on a whisper-yell. "You're right, it's all bullshit, but it sounded good didn't it?"

She gave that some thought. "Yeah, it sounded good. And I don't think any of the guys will see through you the way I do, so you might actually pull off looking like the bigger person."

"Exactly," I declared, feeling triumphant.

We started walking again when Savannah asked, "So, what? You're just going to act all chummy with Luke again even though he's the spawn of Satan?"

"*Pfft*. Hell no! I've got nothing to say to him. I'm just going to act like he doesn't exist and go about my days like he's not even here."

Savannah cut her eyes at me, seeing through my false bravado instantly. "Good plan, Em. There's no *way* that could possibly fail."

She had a point, but whatever. "I see the sarcasm you're throwing, but it's deflecting right off my shield," I replied, snottily.

My plan was far from foolproof, but I'd lived through worse. As far as I was concerned, this was just another bump in the road.

I could totally handle this.

Or so I thought.

MY PLAN TO avoid Luke like the plague was put to the test that same afternoon. It went without saying that I was shocked as hell when he sauntered into the diner, calm as could be. He planted himself at one of the tables, and started browsing through the menu like he didn't have a care in the world. I contemplated refusing service for all of two seconds before I decided to nip this in the bud.

"What do you think you're doing?" I asked as I stomped up to his table. I was *not* going to give in and look at all his well-defined manliness wrapped up nicely in his uniform.

Nope. Not happening. Wasn't going to do it.

"Uh... getting food?" He stared up at me innocently, which

only pissed me off further. He knew I knew exactly what he was playing at, and the fact he thought I was stupid enough not to see through his charade, made me want to stab him with a fork.

Okay, so I might have jumped the gun on accusing Savannah of having too much anger the other day, because I was suddenly right there with her in the whole *ripping Luke a new asshole* thing. I couldn't stand that Luke drove me so mad I was pushed to the point of physical violence. I hadn't been a violent person a day in my life.

"You know I don't want you here. There are other places in town you can eat." I turned on my heels and started away from him. Unfortunately, I didn't get very far. The electric jolt I got from his hand wrapping around my wrist was almost enough to bring me to my knees. Such a simple touch and I felt like I was coming completely undone.

When I turned and looked into his eyes, I was sure the sorrow I saw reflecting in them mimicked my own. "Please." The sincerity in his voice gave me a moment's pause. "I know I don't deserve it after how I left things between us, and I don't expect you to ever forgive me. I just had to come in here and say I'm sorry. I am so, so sorry for everything I did to you, Emmy."

I had no clue how to respond to that. I guess I figured he'd attempt to apologize eventually, I just never thought it would sound so heartfelt. Not knowing how to react I said the only thing that came to mind. "Okay."

His expression was one of complete shock as he took my response in. Luke released my wrist and sat back with a sigh so heavy it sounded like he'd just released the weight of the world. "Thank you."

Apparently, letting him get that off his chest meant more to him than I thought. "I know I'm really pressing my luck, but would you consider letting me eat here?" When I turned my gaze back to him, he had that boyish smile on his face that I had loved so much when we were younger. "It's just that Virgie's has always had the best food. There isn't anywhere halfway decent in a ten mile radius."

It was my turn to sigh. "Fine, you can come in here for lunch or whatever. But I need you to understand something." Placing my hands on the table right beside his, I leaned down and spoke softly enough that only he could hear. "This doesn't mean we're friends. You aren't going to come in here and attempt to chat me up or make bullshit small talk. You want to eat? That's fine. If you're coming in to my diner for any other reason than that, you need to find somewhere else to get your meals. Do you understand?" I only had so much high road in me, and I'd already met my quota for the day by relenting to him eating at my diner.

"I understand," he said quietly. "Just food, I promise."

I stood back to my full height. "Thank you."

He cleared his throat uncomfortably before continuing. "Do you think Virgie would take my head off if I attempted to say hello to her? I haven't seen your Grams around town since I got back."

That question confirmed what I'd known in the back of my mind all along, but it still left me feeling cold and brittle. "You didn't read a single email I sent, did you?" It was hard to speak past the lump in my throat.

This man just couldn't stop hurting me.

He looked down crestfallenly at the scarred table. "No, I didn't."

I stood there and stared, letting the pain of his confession rush through my body as I waited for him to look up at me again. When he finally did, I spoke in a flat, emotionless voice. "You lost the chance to talk to Grams years ago, Lucas. She's dead."

I turned and walked away before he could say anything else.

I'd heard all I wanted to from Lucas Allen.

CHAPTER SIX

EMERSON

PAST

I WOKE to the sun pouring into my room through my window. Remembering the events of the night before, I lifted my arms over my head with a huge smile on my face, stretching out my body and cherishing the dull throb between my thighs that I'd never felt before. Not only had I lost my virginity, but I'd lost it to my best friend in the world. A man that I truly loved.

I turned over to get a glimpse of Luke sleeping in my bed for the very first time only to discover that I was alone. A quick glance around confirmed that he was nowhere to be found. He must have snuck out in the middle of the night, and I could only assume it was because he was worried about Grams coming in and catching us. I reached for my cell on the nightstand to check for messages and was surprised to find that there wasn't a single message from him. Looking at the time and seeing that it was already past ten, I made the decision to call him first. This was our last day together, then he'd be gone for who knew how long. I wanted to be sure to get in as much time with him as possible.

My stomach started to knot with dread when the call went straight to voicemail. Maybe he was asleep. Or maybe his phone had died, and he couldn't find his charger, yet again. I tried to come up with any and every reasonable excuse I could think of, but deep down I had a sinking feeling that something was seriously wrong.

"YOU DID *WHAT?*" Savannah shrieked. I'd just told her about my night with Luke and she was freaking out.

"Will you please calm down?" I whispered anxiously. The last thing I needed was for her mother to overhear our conversation. I grew up in the typical, middleclass suburban neighborhood of Cloverleaf whereas Savannah's family was from the richer part of town. Her mom was already convinced that I was beneath Savannah's social standards, so I didn't need her knowing I lost my virginity to the boy she referred to as white trash when she didn't think we could hear. In all the years I'd known her, I had never been able to figure out where Savannah got her loving nature from.

Her mother was a country club snob who couldn't be bothered, and when her dad wasn't working out of town, he barely remembered he had a daughter. Neither of them had an ounce of the compassion that Savannah did. The only thing I could figure was that she'd somehow been switched up at the hospital, and had gone home with the wrong family. Her real parents were kind and loving, and were out there somewhere, searching for their long lost daughter.

"Calm down? Are you serious! You lose your V-card to your best friend and this is the first I'm hearing about it? I kind of hate you right now."

I collapsed onto her bed as I replayed the night over and

over in my head. "It's not like we'd planned it, Savvy. I know it sounds cliché but it just happened."

"Just happened... Like, it slipped in? You're so full of shit, Emerson Grace! Losing your virginity doesn't *just happen*."

I let out a frustrated huff of air. I was uncomfortable enough simply having to discuss this with Savannah. She certainly wasn't making it any easier with the third degree. I might have been loud mouthed about some things, but when it came to sex, I couldn't talk without turning the color of a cherry tomato. It was humiliating.

"I don't mean it like that! You know what I meant. We didn't go into last night planning on sleeping together. I didn't even think about it happening until he was lying in my bed, holding on to me." I ran my hands through my hair as I tried to put last night into words that would make sense. "It's like it just all clicked into place, you know? I was laying there, missing him like crazy already, and then he climbed through the window, and I just... I just knew."

"So what's that mean for you guys? Are you, like, a couple now? How's that going to work with him going into the Marines?"

I felt the tears pricking the back of my eyes. She was asking the very same questions I'd been asking myself all day. I didn't have any answers, and I desperately wanted some. Unfortunately, the only person who could give them to me had gone radio silent. This despicable apprehension had been knawing at me all day long, and I couldn't seem to shake the feeling that something wasn't right, no matter how hard I tried.

Finally, on a broken whisper, I admitted, "I don't know, Savannah."

She sat down on the bed next to me and wrapped me in her arms. "Hey, come on now. Why are you crying?"

I sniffled and tried my best to pull myself together. "He's not answering any of my calls or texts, Savvy." Saying it out loud made the anxiety even worse. Once it was vocalized, it was no longer just in my head. It was real. "I woke up this morning, and he was gone. Just *gone*. I've tried calling but it keeps going to voicemail." The tears started again, and I was having an even harder time controlling them. "What if he regrets it? He's leaving tomorrow. What if I don't see him again?" The thought of that was quickly sending me into hysterics.

"Hey now, none of that." Savannah started rubbing the back of my hair in soothing motions. "Of course he doesn't regret it."

"How can you know that?" I wanted so badly to believe her, but I just wasn't sure. I had this ache, deep down in the pit of my stomach, telling me something was off, and the more I tried to ignore it, the worse it got. "We've never gone more than a few hours without talking, and now that we've had sex, I can't get a hold of him? That can't be a coincidence."

I could tell that she wanted to believe what she was saying, but her concern was evident. "Well, then screw it," she said with conviction. "If he won't answer his damn phone, then you get your ass over to his house and confront him. He's leaving tomorrow. You need answers, and if you don't get them before then you're going to be miserable. Don't let him leave with any unanswered questions, Emmy. You'll regret it forever."

I knew she was right. I had to talk to Luke face to face, but the thought of that terrified me. "Okay. Yeah, you're right." It was time to suck it up and get some answers.

"Damn straight I am," she declared. After several more minutes of pep talk, I left Savannah's. She hollered after me as I was walking out the door, "Now go over there and kick his ass into gear."

Once I got home, I did something I'd never done in preparation to see Luke. I actually tried. Meaning I went for the full hair and makeup effect. I spent a good twenty minutes on my outfit selection, and I even spritzed on a little perfume. I knew it was ridiculous, but after the night we'd had together, I knew our relationship had changed for good. Gone were the days of just throwing on a ratty pair of sweats and tossing my hair up in a sloppy knot on the top of my head. I wanted Luke to see me as a woman, not the girl he'd grown up with.

I decided on my best pair of dark skinny jeans and my navy and white striped blouse that hung off one shoulder. I paired my outfit with my tan ballet flats, and as I inspected myself in the mirror, I began feeling a little more confident. I managed to tame my wavy, chocolate locks into some semblance of order, and my light blue-gray eyes were accentuated with a soft, shimmery eye shadow. Even I was willing to admit that I looked pretty good, and I was my own worst critic.

All that confidence disappeared at Luke's doorstep. My stomach was a jumbled mess of nerves by the time I opened his front door. Knocking was pointless at Luke's house. His mother—preferring to spend her evenings at whatever bar hadn't kicked her out that week—was never home, and Luke never bothered to lock the door. If someone were to ever knock, he would just holler out that it was open anyway.

The idea of Luke spending his last night at home alone made me sad. Whether or not our relationship went anywhere, I still wanted to be there for him in any way he would let me.

"Luke?" I called out as I stepped over the threshold and into the house. As I moved in further I could hear the sound of muffled voices coming from his bedroom. "Luke?" I called again as I got closer. He didn't respond but the noises were getting louder. A ball of dread formed in the pit of my stomach again.

I was right outside his bedroom door when I heard the distinct moan, and I could tell instantly it wasn't just Luke in there. His door was halfway open, and when I tipped my head to peek in, a piece inside of me withered and died. Tears instantly started streaming down my cheeks, ruining all of the work I'd put into my makeup. Luke was sitting on the end of his bed, pants unbuttoned and unzipped, hanging down around his hips. There was a girl on the floor in front of him, cradled between his knees. I didn't need to be an expert on sex to know *exactly* what they were doing.

Luke's head was thrown back in ecstasy, the muscles in his neck pulled tight as he groaned out "God, Allison, that feels so fucking good. Suck me harder."

"You like that, baby?" she responded in a alarmingly familiar nasally voice.

Allison? He wouldn't do that. I refused to believe it. Luke knew how much I despised Allison Crabtree. She'd made it her life's mission all through high school to make every day a living hell for me. If there was one person on the face of this earth that I could say I truly, irrevocably hated, it would be Allison Crabtree. And Luke *knew* that. He knew how awful she'd been, and how much she tormented me, and there she was, on her knees in Luke's bedroom with his dick down her throat. Only one day after I'd handed him the most precious gift I had to give. The pain hit me like a bullet and radiated through my entire body.

I had to get out of there. I didn't care if they heard me. I hoped they did, and that it put a serious damper on their little party.

Spinning around, I sprinted down the hall as fast as my legs would go, knocking over a small side table in the process. I could barely see through the blur of tears in my eyes, but I was determined not to stop. Once I reached the front door and passed through, I slammed it as hard and I could. I didn't slow down until I reached my front yard. Once there, I realized that the last thing I wanted was for Grams to see me so upset, so I sucked in a huge lungful of air, over and over, trying to get my breathing under control. After we lost my parents Grams had turned into a worrier. It didn't help that with their loss came my uncontrollable dark moods, and I hated the thought of causing her any more distress than I already had. I couldn't let her see me in my current state. Once I was convinced I looked halfway presentable I wiped the tears from my eyes, headed inside.

Grams was in the kitchen making dinner. "Hey, Emmy darlin'. Supper's just about done," she called over her shoulder when she heard me close the front door.

I tried to speak through the knot in my throat and was shocked that my voice came out sounding relatively normal. "I'm not really hungry, Grams," I called out as I headed to my room. "I'm just going to lie down. I think I'm coming down with a cold or something." I *hated* lying to Grams. She'd been such a strong influence in my life for so many years. I respected and loved her with all of my heart, and not being truthful with her ate away at me. But there was no way I could let her see me like this. I couldn't even bring myself to think about what I'd just seen, let alone talk about it. I needed time. Once my head was clear, I would be honest with her.

As soon as I entered my bedroom I headed straight for the attached bath to scrub the ridiculous makeup off my face. Throwing on sweats and tossing my hair back into its signature sloppy knot, I climbed into my bed and cried myself to sleep. Luke had succeeded in doing the one thing no other guy had ever done. He'd managed to completely annihilate my heart in only a matter of seconds. That had to be some sort of record.

By the time I woke the next day he was already gone.

CHAPTER SEVEN

EMERSON

PRESENT DAY

I WALKED into Colt's with Stacia, Savannah, and our other friend Lizzy, all of us sporting our 'I'm with the band' t-shirts. It was tradition for us to come and show support for the guys whenever they played close to home. And just because Luke breezed back into town with all the destruction and devastation of a hurricane, didn't mean I was going to break tradition. These were my boys and I was going to support them.

Jeremy had been playing guitar since he was little, and sometime around sophomore year of high school, he joined forces with Gavin, Brett, and Luke to start a band. After Luke left, the other three kept at it and eventually added Dillon, a guy Jeremy worked with at his body shop. The four have been playing together ever since. They mainly played covers since none of them were any good at song writing, but they still kicked ass, and it was always fun to go to their shows.

We made our way to the front of the crowd by the stage as the guys started setting up. "Hey, check it," Stacia said as she pulled open her purse. Looking in her bag, we spotted a pair of zebra print boy short panties with the tags still on them.

"Um, Stacia, why do you have underwear in your purse? You preparing for a car wreck or something?" I loved all of my friends equally, but Stacia was the girl in the group that always did or said off the wall things. Half the time she didn't make any damn sense, but she provided some much needed comic relief, and we all loved her for it.

I looked up to see her rolling her eyes at me. "*No,*" she responded like what I said was the stupidest thing she'd ever heard. "I bought them to throw on stage to Gavin.

"Wait..." Savannah interrupted. "You *bought* new panties to throw at your boyfriend on stage?"

"Well, yeah. I'm not going to throw my *actual* panties up on stage; that doesn't seem very sanitary. Besides, all my undies are part of a matching set. Throw one pair and I can never wear the bra again. That's just a waste."

"God I love you, girl," Gavin declared from behind Stacia as he wrapped his arms around her waist and kissed her neck. The two of them were a ridiculously cute, only slightly idiotic match made in heaven.

A few minutes later the music started, and the atmosphere in the bar went electric. It was impossible to stay in a bad mood when I was surrounded by good friends, good booze, and great music.

The guys were halfway through their set, and the girls and I were having the time of our lives, shaking our asses and screaming out our undying love and devotion for the band.

I had my eyes closed, and my hands in the air as I moved to the beat and shouted the lyrics to "Carry On Wayward Son" as loud as I could when, all a sudden, the air around me went static. My eyes flew open and my head jerked around of its own accord just as Luke came waltzing through the door of Colt's. It was as if my body had a physical reaction whenever he was within a few feet of me.

Damn traitorous body!

I tried my best not to show any emotion when his eyes met mine but when I caught a glimpse of that bleach blonde, trailer trash slut, Allison Crabtree on his arm all I saw was red... as in blood... as in I was going to cut a bitch. How he could walk into a public place, where he *knew* I was going to be, with that skank beside him was unfathomable.

"Oh no, he did *not* just come in here with that walking advertisement for VD!" Savannah hollered above the music. Sensing that things just got nuclear, my girls flanked me, anxiously waiting for something to go down.

Luke must not have been as detached to my moods as I'd assumed, because he narrowed his eyes at me, tilted his head and studied my expression, then quickly turned and glanced back at Allison. I could see it in his face the moment he realized his colossal mistake.

That's right, buddy. You just screwed up big *time.*

Allison retracted her claws from Luke's arm long enough to head over to the bar and he took that as his opportunity to approach me and my band of killer Barbies. "I like the shirts," he said, pointing in the general area of my chest. My palm actually twitched with the urge to slap him. Talk about him shoving the knife in deeper.

"Yeah, well what can I say? I like to support my true friends whenever I can." My voice was quiet, but no less full of venom. Seeing Allison set me off, and I wanted to take every opportunity to hit him where it hurt, just as he'd done with me.

He actually had the nerve to look at me with remorse in his eyes. "Emmy, can we talk?"

Before I could get so much as a word out, Allison snaked her arm around Luke's waist from behind and plastered her fake boobs to his side, wrapping herself around him like a syphilis infested anaconda. "Hey baby, I got somethin' for you," she said, attempting a sultry voice that came out sounding like baby talk.

I swallowed down the bile rising in my throat and plastered a fake smile on my face. "And I bet I know what it is," I sing-songed. "Just remember Luke, herpes is the gift that keeps on giving." With that I booked it to the bar with Lizzy and Savannah behind me, howling with laughter. Stacia was still by the stage, singing along with Gavin and the rest of the guys. Her attention span rivaled that of a three year old, and the minute I walked away from Luke, she'd forgotten all about our standoff.

"Unbelievable," Lizzy declared. "Like it's not bad enough he's here in the first place, but then he's stupid enough to show up with *her*? Why are men so dumb?"

"A question that will forever plague women the world over," I sighed as I worked hard to keep my gaze from traveling back toward the dance floor.

"I want to claw her eyes out," Savannah told us, positively seething.

Looking over at my friend, an evil smile spread slowly across my face at the visual she just created. "Well, if he's stupid enough to actually approach me, you'll get your chance, Wildcat." For the next half hour I worked diligently to ignore the both of them. But even with all my best avoidance maneuvers, I still wasn't good enough to get away from Luke. He was like a goddamn tractor beam. They must have taught him that shit in the Marines or something, because he eventually managed to corner me at the bar when I'd taken a break from busting a move to order a drink.

"I didn't come here with her, you know." He spit the words out so quickly I almost missed their meaning.

"It's really none of my business, Lucas. You can come here with whomever you want. No accounting for taste, of course."

He rubbed the back of his neck, and I remembered from our childhood that that was something he did when he was extremely nervous. He locked eyes with me again and continued. "I wouldn't do that to you, Emmy. She caught me outside as I was walking in."

If I could have killed him with a look, there was no doubt he'd be lying on the floor in a puddle of blood right then. "You wouldn't do that to me? *Really*? Because I seem to recall, in vivid detail I might add, that you've already done exactly that to me once before." I tried to push him away but he was too strong. It was like trying to move a brick wall.

He wrapped his hand around my arm and towered above me, getting so close we were practically nose-to-nose. "I fucked up. I know that, but I've been trying to talk to you about it since I got back to town." He might have been whispering, but that didn't lessen the menacing growl in his tone. "You haven't given me one fucking chance to explain—"

I cut him off right there. I jerked my arm out of his hold and pushed him back with all my might. I no longer cared about making a scene. *"Explain?"* I yelled louder than I had intended. "You want to fucking explain? You've had eight years to explain, Lucas. Eight. *Fucking. Years!*" I was beyond livid. "I sent you countless emails and letters, giving you every opportunity to *explain*. All you had to do was open them and reply! What is it you want to explain to me, exactly? Is it why I walked into your house and caught you getting sucked off my the girl you *knew* made my life miserable *the day after* you slept with me? You honestly think you've got a good excuse for that?"

When I finally stopped yelling, I noticed that the band had stopped playing and everyone in Colt's was staring in our direction. *"Yes!"* he roared. "I want you to let me fucking explain why I did that!"

"Oh, please," I said, so much sarcasm dripping from those

two words it was a wonder we didn't drown in it. "Let me know what excuse you have that's so good it can fix the damage you caused that night. I'd just *love* to hear it."

He grabbed me by the arm and jerked me through the crowd toward the door. He handled me roughly, but I could still tell that he was holding back his strength, because his firm, demanding grip hadn't hurt me at all.

We made our way out the door and into the parking lot, Savannah, Lizzy, Jeremy and Brett hot on our heels.

"If you don't let her go right now, I'm going to beat the shit out of you!" Savannah hollered. "You might be a Marine, asshole but I've got a fucking black belt in kick-your-ass kwon do. Do *not* test me."

Jeremy was on her in a second. "Shut it, Savannah," he said with more authority than I'd ever heard him use with her. "Let them handle it. Emmy doesn't need you to interfere."

She spun around fast as lightning. "Are you fucking kidding me, Jeremy? Just because you let him sweet talk himself back into your good graces, doesn't mean the rest of us have to buy into his bullshit."

Jeremy's eyes were fierce. It was a look I'd never seen from my carefree, easygoing friend, and it bothered me that I had no idea what the hell was going on in his head. "Savannah, for Christ's sake. For once in your life just *shut the fuck up!* Luke and Emmy need to talk this out without you in the mix. I know how much you love to stick your nose where it doesn't belong, but I swear to Christ, woman, back the hell off."

Holy shit! Savannah was going to cut his junk off and feed it to him. "Are you *insane?*" Savannah's voice had reached a pitch that only bats could hear.

"Maybe, but you know I'm right." I could see Jeremy working to calm his temper. He took Savannah's elbow and started leading her away with the rest of the group following.

"What the hell do you think you're doing?" she asked, losing steam fast. Jeremy had never talked to her or manhandled her like that before, and I knew she was just as startled by the sudden change in his demeanor as I was.

"I'm gonna take your ass home. You won't leave those two alone if you stay here, so I'm not letting you stay."

She didn't even bother to fight back, just let him lead her away. Right before I was yanked back into reality, I recalled thinking that I was so going to get *that* story the following morning. Luke stepped in front of me and blocked my view of my friends' backs. "You going to let me talk now?" he asked.

I rolled my eyes at him. "By all means, speak."

He started pacing and running his hands through that thick black hair. "That night we were together—" he started.

"You mean the night you took my virginity?" I offered snidely, hoping to make him cringe.

"Yes," he hissed out then started pacing back and forth. "You told me you loved me, and after you fell asleep, I was just lying there thinking about how you deserved so much better than me. I knew that if I didn't do something, you'd wait for me. I couldn't let you put your life on hold for me when I knew I wasn't worth it." He stopped pacing and came to stand directly in front of me. "If I'd let you do that, you would have eventually realized what a piece of shit I was, and you'd have regretted it. I couldn't stand the thought of that."

The sudden wave of emotions tangled in my throat made it hard to speak. "You said that I would never lose you. You promised me that." The words came out soft and broken.

He walked up to me and grabbed my face between his hands. The contact was a like a knife to my heart. "I know that, baby girl, and it killed me. Every day for eight years, I thought about how I hurt you. It got so bad that if it hadn't been for a buddy of mine keeping my ass in check while we were in overseas, I probably wouldn't be here now... I can't begin to tell you how much I regret the way I left you." He spoke so quietly I almost couldn't hear him. "I knew you'd come when I wasn't answering your calls. I went and picked Allison up at some party, knowing how much you hated her. I knew if you saw me with another woman, it would be bad enough, but you would never be able to forgive me if you saw me with *her*. I did what I did so that you'd let me go. I wanted you to have the life you deserved. I wanted you to meet someone who was actually worthy of you.

"But what you saw with Allison was fake. After I heard you run out of the house, I pushed her off me and kicked her the hell out. What you saw was never finished, and I *never* had sex with her. I just needed you to let me go, baby girl."

I reached for his hands and pulled them from my face. "You were successful, Lucas," I croaked in a quiet voice. "You wanted to prove you didn't deserve me and you did that...in spades. I know now, more so than I did then, exactly how unworthy of me you actually are."

CHAPTER EIGHT

LUKE

WATCHING Emmy walk away from me in the parking lot of Colt's was one of the worst nights of my life. Staring into her beautiful eyes, the pain and hatred so stark I could feel it, was like dying a thousand times. The one person in my life that I never wanted to hurt was the one I kept hurting over and over again. She was still the most beautiful girl I'd ever laid my eyes on. Those stormy grey-blue depths could always look directly through me and see everything I never wanted her to see. Her hair was still the perfect chocolate brown I remembered, completely natural. It reminded me of melted Hersey's kisses.

Everything about her was pure and untainted. I always thought she was naturally beautiful when we were growing up, and she'd only gotten better with age. I hated putting that sorrow in her eyes, and I didn't have the first fucking clue how to remove it. Everything I said or did was wrong.

I'd spent the past few days beating myself up and getting nowhere. I had been back home for two and a half weeks and had managed to put off the one thing I dreaded doing. Today there was no excuse. I wasn't working. I had no errands to run, and I needed to give Emmy a few more days before I attempted to talk to her again, no matter how badly I wanted to steamroll my way into her life.

My decision was made; I was going to see my mom. I hadn't seen her since moving back, and although we emailed, it was always sporadic. It was time I saw her face-to-face.

I didn't bother knocking, knowing that the door wouldn't be locked. Most of the time she was too drunk to even remember where she put her keys. I opened the door and called out for her. "Ma. You here?"

"In the living room," she called in that raspy smoker voice. Making my way into the living room, I noticed that nothing had changed in the eight years I'd been away. The entryway wall was still covered with my school pictures from elementary all the way through high school. The walls, originally white, were now a gross shade of beige from years of cigarette smoke. I rounded the corner and spotted my mother, sitting on the end of the couch in her bathrobe, cigarette in one hand and a glass in the other. I knew her well enough to know that what was disguised as iced tea was actually one part tea, three parts Jack.

The woman sitting in front of me looked so much older than her forty-six years. The alcohol and smoking had aged her by at least a decade. When I was a child I'd stumbled on some pictures of my mother before my father had entered her life and broken her spirit. I barely recognized the girl in those photographs. She'd been so beautiful once. I got my green eyes and black hair from her. We had the same facial features as well, but it wasn't the outward appearance that concerned me.

Everything I was on the inside, I'd gotten from my dad. That was one of the main reasons I pushed Emmy away like I did. I knew there was a large part of him in me and I couldn't stand to think of her becoming the same broken shell of a woman that my mother had. If Mom hadn't gotten pregnant with me at eighteen, she never would have been stuck with that miserable bastard. She would probably be happy and healthy.

I didn't want to drag Emmy down that same depressing road.

"There's my boy." My mom stood from the couch and walked over to me, wrapping me in a tight hug.

"How you doin', Ma?" I pulled her small frame into mine and squeezed.

"I'm good now that my son's home safe." She looked up at me, her smile so genuine I could see some of the beauty from her past. "I'm so glad you finally had a chance to stop by. I know how busy you've been."

Mom was what you would consider a functioning alcoholic. She's been drinking for so long that, other than some slight slurring and her glassy eyes, you really couldn't tell she was drunk. "I'm sorry I haven't come by sooner."

"Oh, no need to apologize. Come, sit and stay for a while." She led me over to same dingy, out-of-style couch that had been in that living room for as long as I could remember. It was not holding up well. Cigarette burns marred the floral pattern in several places, and it sunk down in the middle where the springs had worn and broken down with time.

Maybe I should buy her a new couch.

"If I'd known you were coming, I would have tried to get to the grocery store to pick something up for dinner."

"No, it's okay, Ma. I'm not going to be able to stay that long anyway."

Her faced dropped, and I instantly felt like the worst son in the world. I knew she'd want to make my coming over a big deal, a homecoming celebration of sort, so I'd intentionally stopped by without advance warning. It's not that I was opposed to her making me a home-cooked meal because I wasn't. Being drunk all day every day never diminished my mother's skills in the kitchen. She still cooked some of the best comfort food I'd ever tasted. I just couldn't stay in this house longer than was absolutely necessary. The memories of the past weighed too heavily, and I could feel them sucking the life right out of me.

"How about you let me take you out to dinner, Ma? It can even be some place fancy where you get all dolled up and I have to wear a jacket and tie." I really did want to spend time with her, just not in this house. Instinct told me she wouldn't take me up on my offer though. Considering the whole town was well aware of the dysfunction that ran rampant in this house, Mom wasn't all that comfortable going out in public.

"Oh sweetie, I'd love to, but I'm feeling a little under the weather right now." I knew exactly what *under the weather* meant for my mother. Some things really hadn't changed at all in the eight years I'd been gone.

I spent a little while longer with Mom before making the excuse that I had errands to run. I hated how strained things were between us, but I wasn't sure if the damage could be undone. There were too many years and too many awful memories to wade through to get to the other side, that most of the time it felt impossible. Of course, I loved her; she was my mother. But I wasn't above admitting I held on to a massive amount of resentment toward her for allowing that angry bastard to make our lives a living hell for so long. For Christ's sake, the bastard had been gone for longer than he was here, and she was still letting him ruin her life.

For the millionth time, I started to think that maybe it was a mistake to move back after so long. There was only so much damage one person could inflict before people couldn't forgive it any longer. Had I reached that point?

The last thing I wanted to do was go back to that empty apartment... *alone*. Eight years ago I'd left behind everyone I ever cared about. Now I was back, living in the town I'd dreamt so many times of escaping, and seeing those people every day, and I'd never felt more alone in my life. Deciding to kill as much time as possible before dragging my ass back to my place and into bed, I stopped off at the store to do some much needed grocery shopping.

Subconsciously, I figured I'd be eating most of my meals at Virgie May's. Since that clearly wasn't going to happen, I needed to buy food. For me, shopping of any kind was akin to torture, and as if being forced to do something I hated wasn't bad enough, when I turned down one of the many aisles, I ran smack into my own personal judge, jury and executioner.

"Well good evening, Deputy Dickweed."

"Savannah," I responded curtly. "Just how many more clever little nicknames you got stored up in that arsenal of yours?"

She scrunched her nose like she was thinking and tapped her chin. "Considering there's a ton of curse words I like that start with "d" I think we've got a while."

"Brilliant."

I tried to push my cart around her, but she sidestepped, blocking me from potential escape. "You shouldn't have come back, you know. Why did you have to come back?" The malice that usually filled her voice when she spoke to me was gone, and in it's place was a sorrow that lanced through me like a white-hot blade. It was almost like whatever pain Emmy felt, Savannah was feeling as well. I could see it clear as day on her face. She was worried.

The only silver lining I could find in this whole fucked up situation was that at least Emmy had someone who loved her that much.

"I appreciate you trying to protect Emmy, Savannah, but the reason's I'm here aren't really your business."

Her expression went hard, despite my effort at a neutral tone. "Why can't you just head back to wherever the hell it is you've been? No one wants you here, Luke. Or are you just too self-absorbed to figure that out?"

Stepping around the cart, I made my way to her, holding my hands up in a gesture of surrender. "Look, I know you hate me, and I get it. I understand. But I came here to make things right. I don't want to cause any more problems. I just want to fix the ones I've already made."

"That's not possible!" she cried. "There's no fixing what you've already done, Luke. Just let it go. Let *her* go. You're going to ruin her all over again!"

For the life of me, I couldn't understand the intensity of her reaction. I felt like I was missing some very crucial pieces to a puzzle. "Jesus Christ!" I finally snapped, losing my cool. "I get that I fucked up, Savannah, but it was eight years ago! How much longer you going make me pay for the sins of my past, huh?"

Something flashed deep in her eyes. It was there and gone before I could figure out what it was I saw. Taking a step back, she looked at me like I was the most disgusting human being on the face of the planet. "What you did was so much more than a simple fuck up," she whispered with so much hatred it was palpable. "She's been through hell, Luke. Absolute hell. There were time when I wasn't sure she'd ever make it out of that fire alive. She finally gets to a point where she can feel happy again, and you breeze back on in and fuck it all up. You can't do that to her again. You need to leave... for Emmy's sake."

Before I could wrap my brain around the bomb she'd just dropped, she was gone, leaving me reeling. I knew that seeing me with Allison all those years ago was going to hurt Emmy, but I never thought it would be to such an extent. I didn't take our night together lightly, at all. I knew she gave me a gift when she asked me to be her first. And it was a gift I'd cherished every moment in the years that passed.

I'd come back to Cloverleaf for one soul purpose, to win my Emmy back. But how long could a woman—or a town for that matter—hold on to that much hatred?

CHAPTER NINE

EMERSON

"OKAY, woman, you better start spilling right now." Savannah and I were taking full advantage of a rare lazy day. Lying out on my back deck in shorts and tank tops, we worked on our tans while drinking the batch of margaritas I'd just blended. It was the perfectly refreshing drink to stave off the sometimes brutal Texas heat.

Savannah lifted the margarita glass to her lips and too a healthy sip of the icy liquid. "I don't know what you're talking about," she replied, biting the inside of her cheek to hide the grin that was fighting to break free.

"Like hell, you don't. What happened to you after Jeremy dragged you away the other night?" It had been a few days since my latest public scene with Luke at Colt's, and this was the first time I'd been able to nail Savannah down long enough to get the scoop.

"What makes you think something happened?" She started gnawing on her bottom lip, so I knew there was a story there, and Savannah was intent on making me drag it out of her.

"Uh... because I know you."

She took another gulp before spitting out in rapid fire,

"Ibroughthimhomeandwehadsex." The sentence fell out of her mouth so fast I could have sworn I misunderstood. I *prayed* I misunderstood.

"I'm sorry, *what*?" I asked in shock.

"Oh shut up! You heard me, don't act like you didn't."

"Savannah!" I scolded. The gossip mill in out little town was already running rampant with Lucas Allen's return. Now Cloverleaf was at risk of being hit by the tornado I'd lovingly nicknamed "Jervannah". The two of them together was disaster just waiting to happen. And lord only knew how many people would be taken out in its wake.

"What? Why do you automatically assume this is a bad thing? What if we got back together or something?"

I twisted in her direction and started ticking the reasons off on my fingers. "First, I know you two didn't get back together, because when I saw him today, he didn't have a perma-grin. Secondly, you didn't call me from the bathroom *right* after it happened to tell me all about it, in sweaty, gory detail. Third—"

"Okay, okay," she interrupted. "I get your point, jerk-face. We didn't get back together."

I dropped my head into my hands. "Ohhh, this is going to be so bad."

"Why does it have to be bad? Why can't things just go back to normal?" She knew better than to ask a question that. She was grasping at straws.

"Because you know him, Savannah. You know exactly how he's going to get. He's going to hold on to this for a few days, thinking he's got a chance at getting you back, and when he realizes that's not going to happen, he's going to get all butt hurt and walk around in a perpetual state of pissed right the hell off. There'll be silent treatment, then public blow ups and potential physical fighting once you get pissed off to the point of punching the shit out of him." *All things I'd seen from the two of them before.* I wanted those two back together almost as much as Jeremy did, but not this way. Savannah wasn't ready and that was going to destroy him. I couldn't stand the idea of Savannah doing something that couldn't be undone. My heart broke for both of them. For Jeremy, because his heart was about to get stomped on, yet again. And for Savannah, because for some reason, she was intent on continuing her self-destructive tendencies. There was nothing worse than standing idly by while your best friend made one bad decision after another, but she wouldn't talk to you or let you help.

"Well, what the hell did you expect me to do? Did you *see* him the other night? He's never talked to me like that before. Hand to God, Emmy. I about had an orgasm when he went all alpha like that." It was another classic example of Savannah acting without thinking about the repercussions.

I rolled my eyes playfully. "Ugh. You've got serious problems."

"Admit it," she teased. "It was totally hot. Who knew he had that in him?"

"Fine!" I admitted in defeat. I threw myself back down on my lounge chair and crossed my arms over my chest indignantly. "It might have been just a *little* sexy seeing him go all he-man on your ass."

"Thank you!" she declared victoriously.

"Savannah," I started, getting very serious. This wasn't a joking matter. "You're going to break that man. You know how he feels about you. Keeping him on a string like this is just cruel. You can't keep giving him false hope, sweetie."

"I'm not stringing him along," she demanded.

"You are..."

Before I could finish my sentence, she was on her feet and sliding into her flip flops. "Why don't you just stay out of my shit and take care of your own, Emmy! This is none of your business."

I jumped up and followed after her as she headed to the gate that led to my driveway. I couldn't let her leave mad. "Wait a minute. I didn't mean to upset you, Savvy. I'm just worried."

"I don't need you worrying about me, Emmy. I'm a grown-ass woman and I'm more than capable of taking care of myself. You're not my mother."

She was at her car with her keys in her hand by the time I caught up with her. I was thoroughly confused at the turn of events. Savannah might have been prone to dramatics, but she was far from sensitive. She had her outbursts mainly because our little town could get pretty boring at times. Savannah said she behaved the way she did as a public service, it provided the townspeople with some much needed entertainment. So her sudden behavior was more than a little surprising. "I'm not trying to mother you. You're my family. I care what happens to you."

That took some of the wind out of her sails. Her shoulders visibly drooped and she took a deep breath. "Look, I'm just in a shitty mood right now, okay. Maybe I'm PMSing, or something," she said, trying to make light of everything that had just happened. "I'm sorry I took it out on you."

I went to her, wrapping my arms around her waist and pulling her into a hug. "Hey, it's all good. Just don't be mad at me, okay? I hate it when you're mad at me."

She returned the hug just as tightly. "I'm not mad. I'm just going to head home. I'm not really in a margarita kind of mood anymore."

I knew she wasn't okay, but I also knew if I pushed her any further things could get even worse. So I just let her go. Standing in my driveway, I watched her car disappear around the corner, wondering to myself just what the hell was going on with the people in my life. And how was I going to help fix it?

THE NEXT MORNING I was standing behind the counter at Virgie May's, stocking the pastry cabinet when I felt a pair of arms come around my waist and a body bang into my back. "I'm sorry about yesterday," Savannah spoke with her face buried between my shoulder blades. This was just one of the many reasons why I loved her so much. We both hated it when our relationship was strained in any way. We loved each other so much that I wasn't surprised she was hugging me and apologizing less than twenty-four hours later.

"I was a bitch and I hate fighting with you," she continued.

I reached behind me and wrapped my arms around her as best I could, and squeezed her back. "We aren't fighting. It was just a little disagreement. And if you keep calling my best friend a bitch, I'll kick your ass."

We released each other, and I turned to face her. "We cool?" she asked.

"We're always cool. And I promise I won't give you anymore shit about Jeremy." What happened between them still bothered me, but I was willing to ignore the impending doom in order to make Savannah happy. She'd done so much for me. It was the least I could do in return.

"Love you."

"Love you, too. Now, enough of this sappy Hallmark crap. I'm short a waiter so you're up."

She reached under the counter and grabbed an apron as she grumbled, "Sonofabitch. I knew I should've waited for you to close up before apologizing."

CHAPTER TEN

EMERSON

PAST

"HOLY SHIT. Holy shit, holy shit, *holy shit!* Savannah, what the hell am I going to do?" I was hyperventilating. My vision was starting to go black. *Shit!* I was going to pass out.

"Just relax, honey. Maybe it's wrong. How many of these did you pee on?" Savannah picked up one of the sticks sitting on the bathroom counter and compared it to the directions on the back of the box.

"Six, Savvy. I peed on six sticks and all of them say the same damn thing. *Positive!*"

This couldn't be happening. I couldn't possibly be pregnant. I'd had sex with *one* person, *one* time, and I got pregnant? Obviously, I really pissed someone off in a past life and was paying for it in this one.

"Calm down, Emmy. Try to breathe." That was easy for her to say. She didn't just find out she'd been knocked up by a guy that ran out on her the morning after, then disappeared from her life all together.

"How the hell am I supposed to calm down? I'm a pregnant college freshman whose baby daddy ran off to parts unknown and I have no freaking clue how to get a hold of him! OhmyGod... I'm a *statistic*! I'm the girl we had to watch in that public service video in health class last year!"

Savannah started pacing around the small dorm room muttering to herself. "If I ever see that piece of shit again, I'm going to cut his dick off and shove it down his throat!"

Savannah was the one who sat with me for weeks while I cried into a gallon of chocolate chip cookie dough ice cream. She was the one who had held me up when I was at my worst. Luke left for basic the morning after I saw Allison Crabtree going down on him like giving a blowjob was a freaking Olympic event. I swallowed my pride—probably like Allison swallowed other things—and tried emailing him a few times, only to get absolutely nothing in response. He'd gone off the grid. But he didn't just cut me off. He wasn't talking to Jeremy, Brett or Gavin either. The longer he avoided them, the madder they got. When they eventually found out about this, shit was going to hit the fan.

Savannah was the president and founder of the I Hate Lucas Allen fan club. If someone hurt me, by association they hurt her. And Savannah was *not* one to forgive easily.

I wasn't sure if it was hormones, or the fact that my life was going down in a big steaming pile of crap, but I chose that moment to break down. I cried for the situation I was in. I cried because the guy I loved didn't love me back, and had left me behind. I cried for the baby I was carrying. I cried because I had no freaking clue what I was going to do.

It was the big, ugly kind of crying too. The snot-coming-out-of-your-nose, big-red-blotches-on-your-cheeks, swollen-eyes kind of crying.

Savannah just sat with me on the floor and rubbed my back

until I got it all out. "How the hell am I supposed to tell Luke? He won't respond to my emails. He never answers when I call his cell phone. I don't even have an address to send a goddamned hand written letter!"

She grabbed my cheeks in her hands and stared into my eyes. "You do what you can, babe. Send him an email and try calling. If he doesn't reply to anything, there's nothing else you can do."

"Nothing else I can do. *God*, I'm going to be a single mom," I whispered, beneath a fresh wave of tears.

After several more hours and *a lot* more sobbing, we sat together in front of my laptop. I drafted about three thousand different versions of the email to Luke before I was somewhat satisfied with it. Savannah and I both agreed that it wasn't right to drop that kind of bomb on him in an email. By cell phone wasn't much better, but it was the best option in a list of shitty options. I hit the Send button on the email I'd spent so long drafting. I asked that he call me as soon as possible, or at least pick up when I called him. I told him I had some very important news I needed to tell him about. I drew the line on begging and telling him I loved him. I made those simple requests and kept it at that. My anger was so raw, my pride so beaten and bruised, that I'd have rather raised our baby completely on my own than grovel to that man.

Three days later, I hadn't gotten a reply. No email. No phone call. I allowed myself only one call a day for those three days. I made a deal with myself that I wasn't going to leave it in a voicemail. I could just see that going well, *Hey there stranger. Guess what, you knocked me up, daddio... Call me back...*

"Fuck him," Savannah clipped from her sprawled out position on my bed. "If he's too big of a jerk to respond or call back when you've told him you need to talk to him, then that's his own damn problem. You don't need to bust your ass trying to tell him something he obviously doesn't want to hear."

"Is it totally pathetic that, even though I knew he wouldn't answer, I still hoped?"

"No. That's not pathetic. You are *not* pathetic."

I was so tired of crying by that point. It left me feeling weak and needy. And I *hated* feeling that way. I always tried so hard not to depend on anyone else for my happiness because I knew from experience that could be taken away in a blink of an eye. The fact that Luke's lack of response affected me so deeply was turning me into a woman I didn't want to be. "What am I going to do?"

Savannah stood in front of me with her hands on her hips, looking determined. "You aren't going to do anything alone. *We* are going to get through this. I'm going to be here every step of the way. You're having this baby, and I'm going to be there right by your side, helping you raise it."

That only made me cry even harder. "I am so damn lucky to have you."

"Of course you are. And I'm lucky to have you. We're in this together, honey, you as Mommy, me as cool Auntie Savvy."

"Auntie Savvy. I like that." Savannah never stopped trying to make me feel better. She had her own life and didn't need the drama I was bringing into it, but she never blinked when it came to helping me. She was consistently solid.

"Me too. It has a nice ring, doesn't it?" We laughed, and she helped me fix my face so that we could go out for some much needed retail therapy. We were shopping with one thing in mind... baby supplies. Our first stop was the bookstore to buy any baby book that looked the slightest bit helpful. We bought two copies of everything since Savannah was determined to learn everything she needed to learn to help me with my baby. From how she was acting you would have thought Savannah was preparing to deliver the baby all on her own, if necessary.

She joked that she was going to make a kickass daddy, and my heart opened up even more.

THE FURTHER ALONG I got into the pregnancy, the harder things became. My morning sickness was more like all-day sickness, and it didn't end after the first trimester like it was supposed to. The baby was growing and healthy, but my doctor wasn't happy with the amount of weight I was losing. If it wasn't nausea, it was wicked heartburn. If it wasn't heartburn, it was dizzy spells. I was so sick that I ended up getting too far behind in my classes and couldn't keep up. I made the incredibly hard decision to leave college and move back home, hoping I'd be able to start taking classes again once the baby was born. It wasn't easy to put my education on hold, but the little peanut I was carrying around meant more to me than anything else.

I put my foot down when Savannah informed me she was dropping out too. There was no way I was letting her give up her education just to move back with me. Those arguments got pretty heated, and I ended up telling her that the only way I'd allow her to help me with the baby was if she stayed in school. She finally relented, but not without a fight first.

Time passed, and each day was yet another day I didn't hear from Luke. Finally, I decided it was time to give up on him, and I was surprisingly all right with that decision. Even though this pregnancy was making me sick as a dog, I couldn't possibly be unhappy. I had this little person growing inside me. This little being that—even though it looked like a tiny little reptile in the ultrasound pictures—I was already totally in love with. I couldn't even find it in me to continue my hatred of Luke. He might be an asshole, but without him I wouldn't have had this precious little gift. Every day I woke up, I'd put my hand on my belly and tell my baby "Mommy loves you so much". Everything was going to end up fine.

CHAPTER ELEVEN

EMERSON

PRESENT DAY

MY FRIENDS WERE rock stars when it came to birthdays. We considered each other family and made sure to have a huge blow out when each person's birthday rolled around. It was Gavin's month so we decided to host at Stacia's since he was her boyfriend, but mainly because she was the only one who had a house and backyard big enough to hold so many people. Invitation was spread by word of mouth, so basically the whole town was invited. And most everyone had shown up.

The party was in full swing as I headed back into Stacia's kitchen to mix up some more French onion dip. Standing at the sink, my back was to the doorway when the air around me started to crackle. I glanced over my shoulder and saw Luke standing there, watching me like a predator would watch its prey. He was leaning up against the doorframe with his arms crossed over his barrel chest, looking sexier than he had any right to be. The olive green Henley brought out the color in his eyes, and looked fantastic stretched across his muscled frame.

As my gaze traveled further south I took in the supremely faded, soft looking jeans that hugged him to perfection. Never in my life had I so badly wanted to be a pair of jeans.

I gave my head a vicious shake to get my thoughts out of the gutter. *He's not hot,* I told myself. *You hate him, you hate him... just remember that!* "You need any help?" he asked me as he pushed off the wall and started in my direction.

I turned back around and stared at the bowl of dip like it was the most fascinating thing I'd ever seen. "No, I'm just about done here. The party's out back, you can just walk on through."

I closed my eyes against the sudden onslaught of memories that came when his scent invaded my senses. Fresh, clean cotton mixed with the woodsy fragrance of the outdoors. It was a scent I'd once known so well. It was one that used to give me comfort, but now all it did was remind me of how badly my heart had been broken. "Okay. I guess I'll see you out there." His voice was laced with disappointment, but I wouldn't allow myself to turn and acknowledge it.

I released the breath I hadn't realized I was holding when I heard the sliding door shut behind him. It took me several minutes longer than it should have to mix a packet of French onion soup in with a tub of sour cream, but I needed any stall tactic I could find. Unfortunately, making dip wasn't rocket science, so I was already done. I sucked in a fortifying breath, grabbed the bowl and headed out the door. Luke was already sitting in a lawn chair by Jeremy, Gavin, Stacia and Brett. Savannah was standing off to the side in conversation with Lizzy and a few other people, but she was multitasking like a pro, and staring daggers at Luke at the same time.

Jeremy and Gavin seemed to have moved forward with Luke, but I noticed that Brett didn't look happy that he was there either. It wasn't something I wanted to admit, but I felt a little guilty that some my friends were refusing to forgive him.

Luke had been home for over a month, and even though I couldn't find it in myself to forgive him, it bothered me that Brett and Savannah still harbored so much animosity. Once upon a time we'd all been such close friends. It didn't seem right that they weren't more receptive to his apologies. It was hypocritical of me to want them to forgive him considering I hadn't. The reasonable part of me knew that. They felt the way they did because of me and if I couldn't forgive him, who was I to expect them to? Still, this didn't sit well with me.

I walked over and sat the bowl down on the table near Savannah. "Sweetie, you can put the bitch away for the night. He's here for Gavin's birthday, not to start anything."

Savannah rolled her eyes before responding. "This isn't me being a bitch, Emmy. This is me every day of the week, and you know it."

"I do, you're right. And I love you anyway." I pulled her into a hug then grabbed her and Lizzy's hands and dragged them to the circle with the rest of our friends, where I took a seat next to Brett. Refusing to sit by Luke, Savannah sat between me and Stacia, leaving Lizzy to take the seat next to him. I didn't miss her glare at Savvy and as she mouthed *bitch*, to which Savannah just smiled.

"So what are we talking about?" I asked, taking the very first steps in the direction to fix the rift between everyone.

AS THE NIGHT went on and no drama unfolded, I started to relax and really enjoy myself. Luke and I hadn't really engaged each other in conversation, but that didn't stop us from getting into the stories other people were telling. Everything seemed to be going great, and I had slowly started to lower my guard.

This, of course, was a mistake. Because as soon as I did,

Allison 'Bitchface' Crabtree came sauntering into the backyard looking like she'd been rode hard and put up wet.

"What the hell?" Stacia demanded. It was strange, hearing that tone come out of her mouth. Stacia had always been such a sweet, soft-spoken girl growing up and that hadn't changed as we got older. But the situation definitely warranted her sudden spike of anger. Allison *never* attended one of our parties. She always acted like she was too good for them, but the truth was, she hadn't been welcome. This was the problem with not sending formal invites to these things. Any old street walker could just come wandering up.

I shouldn't have been surprised. With Luke back in town, Allison started showing up to a lot of places where she wasn't wanted. Tonight was no different. She made her way over to him, shaking her ass provocatively, and wrapped her arms around Luke's neck. Brett placed his hand on my knee and give it a squeeze. I glanced in his direction and gave him a small smile, then grabbed his hand and twined his fingers with mine. I wanted him to know how much his support meant to me.

The instant Luke realized who was molded to his body he took her arms and pulled them away from his neck. Undeterred, Allison grabbed an empty lawn chair and shoved it rudely between him and Lizzy. "So how's it going?" Allison asked the group collectively. She had no interest in holding a conversation with us, but she was at least smart enough to know she had to play nice in front of Luke if she wanted to stay on his good side.

However, Savannah wasn't about playing nice. "Bitch, what the hell do you think you're doing here?"

I grabbed for her arm to keep her in her seat. The last thing this party needed was a brawl. "I'm here for Garrett's party."

"Gavin," Stacia hissed through clenched teeth. One of the only things that could provoke soft-spoken Stacia was an insult directed toward her boyfriend, Then the claws came out, and trust me when I say, they were sharp as knives.

"Whatever," Allison said with a flick of her wrist. "Luke invited me, so I figured I'd stop by."

I wanted to murder him on the spot, but Luke's eyes shot to mine and I saw the confusion and worry crashing like violent waves in their green depths. "Hold up, I never invited you, Allison. You asked what I was doing tonight, and I told you I was going to a party. That's not an invite." His voice held so much conviction that I actually believed him.

"Well, I knew what you meant, baby," she cooed, so oblivious to the mounting discomfort at her presence I almost felt sorry for her. It had to hurt to be that clueless.

Turning her head in Luke's direction, Allison caught him looking in my way. I watched, my stomach plummeting to the ground, as a vicious smile crept across her lips. "Emerson, should you really be drinking?" The fake concern dripping from her unnaturally plumped lips made me sick.

In that very moment I wanted nothing more than to punch her in her stupid, bitchy face. Sometimes being the bigger person really sucked. "Aren't you an alcoholic or addict or something?" I didn't miss the collective gasp that came from the group, or the fact that Luke was staring at me in bewilderment.

"No, I'm neither, Allison, but I appreciate your concern." I gave her my brightest smile. "Since we're sharing and caring, I feel that I should tell you something." I leaned forward, pasted a serious look on my face and pointed down at her drink. "Maybe you should switch to light beer. Your thighs are starting to look a little chunky in your hooker skirt."

Who wears a leather mini skirt and sequined halter top to a backyard barbeque anyway?

I wasn't going to stick around to see what she had to say next. I stood up and started for the sliding door. "Where are you going?" Savannah called after me.

I turned back and looked at my friends, while simultaneously avoiding Luke eyes. "You know I love you guys, and I'm sorry to bail on your birthday, Gavin, but this party just went downhill fast. I think I'll bail before animal control shows up to collect the strays." I shot one last glare in Allison's direction then tried to make as graceful an exit as possible.

My hopes of that were demolished when Jeremy's boom command vibrated through the air, "All of you. Kitchen. Now!"

Gavin, Luke, and Stacia stood and headed toward the back door with Brett and Lizzy following behind. Savannah defiantly kept her ass in her seat, lasers shooting from her eyes in Jeremy's direction. A second later Lizzy grabbed her elbow and yanked her up. When Allison was stupid enough to try and follow us, Jeremy nipped that in the bud. "What do you think you're doing? Just because you're panting after Luke's jock doesn't make you a part of this group. You are *not* part of this group. You're welcome to leave at any time. Preferably at this very minute." He turned and stomped into Stacia's house, dismissing Allison completely. I couldn't hold back the giggle that escaped when I saw the expression on her face.

None of us got the chance to say anything before Jeremy jumped right in, feet first. "This bullshit has to stop," he said. "This group, right here, is a family. We need to find a way to move past this, because this shit's breaking us. We've got people going at each other's throats, people bailing on parties, people taking sides... Just stop already!"

We all dropped our eyes to the floor like a bunch of naughty children being disciplined. Even Savannah had the decency to look guilty.

"Now this shit started between Emmy and Luke, and it needs to stay between them. It's not our place to get into their business. Don't give me that look, Savannah," he snapped before she got a chance to interrupt. He turned back to Luke and me.

"Do y'all think I'm wrong?" he asked us both.

"No," we replied at the same time.

"Honestly," I started, shifting my gaze to each of my friends, keeping my eyes on Brett and Savannah longer than the others. "I love you all. And Jeremy's right, we're a family. My issues with Luke need to stay between us. I can't stand seeing everyone divided because you guys feel like you need to take sides." I looked over at Luke, and was shocked to find him smiling at me. We weren't on our way to being friends, but maybe we could at least find a common ground after this. "Will it work for everyone if Luke and I make a deal right now to be civil with each other when we're all out together?"

Relief swelled through the entire group.

Luke walked over to me and extended his hand. "I can work with that if you're comfortable with it."

My attention flicked to his hand before lifting back up to his eyes. "Works for me," I said taking his hand. Ignoring the zing that shot through my body at the contact, I sealed my fate by saying, "You got a deal."

CHAPTER TWELVE

EMERSON

I WAS ALREADY dead on my feet, and it was barely ten in the morning.

The diner was in the middle of the breakfast rush, with the early service patrons having just wandered in after church. I knew things weren't going to slow down until well after lunch, but I hadn't had a good night's sleep in ages. Since Luke showed back up my mind kept wandering to the past, which was not a good place for it to be. Both of us were trying hard to keep our word and get along when in the same place for the sake of our friends, but that didn't make seeing him any easier. I was so exhausted, I just wanted to go home, crawl in my bed and sleep for at least twenty-four hours.

I was so out of it that I didn't even notice the handsome man sitting at the table I was standing at. I'd worked as a waitress for so long that taking orders was second nature. I was able to jot down a complete order without really noticing the person placing it. Normally, on days like this, I considered that a gift. That was not the case with this guy.

When I finally took notice of the man in front of me, I instantly got lightheaded. He was, by far, one of the best looking men I'd ever seen. If put in a line up with Luke, this guy would have come in a *very* close second. I normally preferred my guys to be extremely tall, dark and handsome. This guy had the tall and handsome down but was lacking the dark, which didn't take away from his total hotness. One. Damn. Bit.

Although he was sitting, I guessed he stood at 6'2, probably closer to 6'3, and was built like a brick shithouse. There wasn't a single solitary place on his body not packed with muscle... at least from what I could see. He looked like he skipped shaving that morning, so his strong, square jaw was deliciously scruffy. His sandy, dark blond hair had that rumpled style that looked like he'd just gotten laid. For all I knew, he had, but that was none of my business. I'd always been a fan of ink on guys, and I could see the makings of an intricate design on his right upper arm, sneaking out the sleeve of his tight gray t-shirt. I noticed he had the Eagle, Globe, and Anchor symbol etched on his left forearm with Semper Fi in bold lettering underneath, indicating he was a Marine. I'd always had a thing for men in uniform... what woman doesn't? But since Luke, I'd kind of had an aversion to military men. I was happy to say that blondie had cured me of said aversion.

Damn, he's sexy.

When I finally drew my gaze back up to his face, I noticed the most stunning pair of aquamarine eyes. I couldn't recall ever seeing eyes such a unique shade of blue. They were almost teal. It was easy to see the grin in them. I'd been busted. Marine hottie just caught me checking him out. Instead of allowing myself to be embarrassed, I owned it and plastered on my best smile.

"What can I get you today?" I asked.

His grin turned into a full blown smile, and *damn*, was it a fine smile! "Well, I don't know." I caught a twinge of a southern accent, but it didn't sound like he was from Texas. It had more of a Louisiana drawl to it. "I'm new in town so this is my first time eating here. What would you recommend, *cheri*?"

Ooh, cheri. *Yum. Yep, definitely Louisiana.*

I wasn't afraid to admit it. I totally swooned. "Well, seeing as I own this place and I know for a fact that everything on the menu is delicious, I'd say you can't go wrong with anything. But if I was forced to choose, I'd go with the buttermilk pancakes."

"So you're Virgie May?" he asked with a cheeky grin.

"Not exactly."

"Hmm," he mumbled, scratching his scruffy chin as he looked back at his menu. "Bacon or sausage?"

"Sausage. Definitely," I replied with a smile.

"Okay. Scrambled or fried up?"

I gave a little giggle. "Sunny side up, all the way."

He banged his hand down on the tabletop. "Well alright then, sounds delicious. But I can't help but wonder... does that meal come with your number by any chance?"

Oh, this guy was slick. I threw my head back in laughter. "It most certainly doesn't. But I'll tell you what." I pointed down to the tattoo on his forearm. "Seeing as you're a Marine and all, the meal's on the house. That's the best I can do."

He placed his hand over his heart as if he was hurt. "You wound me, *cheri*," he said with a sly grin.

"Somehow I doubt that."

"So does your man realize how lucky he is to have such a beautiful woman on his arm?"

I leaned down and rested my palm on his table. "No man, but thanks for the compliment."

He threw me another mega-watt smile, showing his gleaming white teeth. "No man, huh? So you're saying I got a chance."

I couldn't help but laugh again. This guy was too much. "I

said no such thing, Marine! Boy, you're relentless, aren't you?"

He was just about to respond when I heard a sound from over my shoulder that couldn't be described as anything other than an animalistic growl. "What the hell's going on here?"

I turned to see Luke, looking positively outraged. *Well this isn't going to help our agreement out any* I thought as I looked into his enraged, green eyes. "Just helping a customer, Lucas. Nothing to get your panties in a twist over." McHottie Marine's back was to Luke, so I didn't miss the irritation in his eyes as he turned to face him, no doubt about to cause some trouble. So you could imagine my shock when a surprised smile slowly spread over Luke's face as he said, "Well, I'll be damned. What the fuck are you doing in Cloverleaf, you piece of shit?" Blondie was now standing directly in front of Luke, and the two of them wrapped each other in a man hug, complete with the typical hard pound on the back.

"I remembered you always talking about this town, so I figured I'd come see what all the fuss was about. I was just chatting up this pretty little thing here when you rudely interrupted us." He turned his attention back to me as he extended his hand. "I don't believe we formally met. Trevor Devareau. It's nice to meet you."

I politely placed my hand in his and shook, feeling the crushing weight of disappointment. It wasn't like I actually planned on giving him my number, but it was nice to have an attractive guy flirt with me. I'd been out of the game for so long. But finding out he was a friend of Luke's killed the excited butterflies that had taken flight in my belly just minutes ago. "Emerson Grace. Welcome to Cloverleaf."

"So how do you know Luke here?"

"No story there, really. We just used to know each other." I cut my eyes to Luke just in time to see his jaw tick with agitation at my answer.

"Emmy and I were best friends growing up," he offered, as if the answer I had provided hadn't been good enough.

Recognition flashed across Trevor's face. "Wait... Emmy? You're Emmy?" I gave a confused nod before he looked back at Luke. "Dude, I had no clue this was *your* Emmy. I never would have made a play for her had I known."

What. The. Fuck? "Uh, excuse me, but I am most definitely *not* his Emmy." I scribbled out his order on a ticket slip, slapped it on the table and started to walk away.

"What's this?" he called to me, holding the ticket in his hand.

"It's your check," I replied dryly.

"I thought Marines ate free."

I turned back to face Trevor and Luke head on, cocking a hip out to one side. "They do," I replied in a snarky tone. "But there are two types of Marines in Cloverleaf. I held up my index finger. "There are regular Marines who don't pay to eat at Virgie May's." I held up my middle finger next. "Then there are the Marines that are friends with Luke. They have to pay to eat." I spun back around and headed to the kitchen, throwing over my shoulder, "And that doesn't cover the cost of a tip." I pushed through the kitchen door just in time to hear Trevor burst out laughing as he informed Luke, "Dude. I think I'm in love."

That little scene wasn't exactly me trying to be civil toward Luke, but what could I say. The first guy who'd hit on me in forever turned out to be a friend of his.

Talk about a shot to the ego.

CHAPTER THIRTEEN

LUKE

"I'M glad to see you man, but I'm just gonna say this once. Emmy is off limits."

Trevor held up his hands in surrender. "Hey man, no worries. She's a cutie and all, but now that I know who she is, I'm backing off."

An immediate sense of relief crashed over me like a wave. "Good. I've got enough going against me with that girl as it is."

"So what's the deal with you two? I mean, you talked about her so much that I feel like I know her already. What's with the ice queen act?"

There was a possibility that I'd left some pretty damn important things out when I told Trevor about my life. "It's a long story. Let's just say I made some mistakes before leaving town, and I don't know if that shit can be undone."

Emmy must have seen me sit down in front of Trevor because she returned with a carafe of hot coffee. "You staying long enough for a cup?" she asked. Her tone wasn't exactly polite, but at least she was acknowledging my existence.

"Yeah, if it's okay with you?"

She sat a cup in front of me and began to fill it. "Fine

by me."

She quickly turned and walked away after filling my cup. It was a douche move, but one I couldn't control. I stared at her ass as she walked away. She still had the best ass of any woman I'd ever seen.

I turned back and saw that Trevor had caught me. With a smirk on his face, he asked "From how you used to talk, I assumed you were pretty tight before you left."

"Yeah, we were." I picked up my cup and savored the dark, rich flavor. Virgie May's still had the best coffee I'd ever had the luxury of drinking.

"So what happened?" He sounded casual, but I knew better. He was the nosiest bastard on the planet. He'd rival every female in Cloverleaf when it came to gossip.

"Not a conversation we should have here, brother. I'll fill you in later. For now, why don't you tell me how you ended up in my town?"

"No big reason, just needed a change of scenery."

"Uh, huh." I'd known Trevor long enough to be able to read when there was more to the story than what he'd been giving me. "Let me guess. There's a husband after your ass for banging his wife?" Trevor was a good guy but he wasn't exactly picky with who he took to bed. All a woman needed to get Trevor's attention were good looks, a pulse, and an understanding that once the sun came up their fun was over.

"Nah, no husband involved."

"So it must be a *Fatal Attraction* scenario then."

"Dude, you've got no idea," he said. Trevor rubbed his face with both hands before explaining. "We're talking stage-five clinger, man. This chick takes crazy to a whole new level."

"I told you, brother. One of these days your dick was gonna get you in trouble."

"Is it my fault I'm hung like a horse?"

That wasn't a visual I needed before breakfast. "Maybe not. But it is your fault that you'll stick it in anything that makes eye contact."

"Whatever. Can I at least count on you for a place to crash since moral support isn't in your vocabulary?"

The idea of having a roommate was kind of appealing. I'd spent way too much time by myself since moving back. My thoughts weren't something I wanted to depend on for company. "Yeah, man, I got you. My place isn't all that great, but it's got an extra room and a bed."

Trevor picked up his coffee and took a drink. "That's all I need." Putting the cup down, he picked up his check and looked at me. "You think she's serious about paying?"

"Oh yeah, she's serious." A waitress came and sat a plate of pancakes down in front of Trevor. He glanced up at her and smiled, and she instantly blushed at his attention. This wasn't anything I wasn't used to. All Trevor had to do was flash a grin and women's panties everywhere melted. That didn't mean I wanted to see it. I cleared my throat to get the waitress's attention. I didn't recognize her, but that didn't mean anything... I'd been gone for a long time, there were a ton of new people in town I hadn't known before I left. "You think I could get some pancakes?" I asked.

"Sure thing, Deputy. Emmy already put in your order, should be just a few minutes."

Well, that was promising. She might have thrown some attitude my way when I first got in, but the fact she put in an order for my favorite breakfast showed that she was still sticking to our agreement. No way in hell I was counting on getting my meal for free, though.

"Damn," Trevor said with a groan. "She wasn't joking, these are the best pancakes I've ever had."

"I know, that's why you have to pay your check. Emmy

won't hesitate to ban you from this fine establishment. And trust me, that's the last thing you want. I just got my privileges back. I've been eating shitty frozen meals for weeks now." I trembled at the thought of ever having to go back to those fucking Mighty Man Meals again.

"Well, I'd be golden if it wasn't for you. She'd already offered to comp my food until you showed up. I've been here half an hour, and you've already managed to screw me over."

The waitress delivered my plate and I immediately dug in. "Hey, asshole. I didn't tell you to fuck a nutcase and use Cloverleaf as your hideout."

Trevor laid his fork and knife down and leaned in. His eyes cutting from left to right, as if he was looking for someone. "Don't even joke about that. This is serious shit. I'm almost scared to go to sleep at night. I keep thinking that I'm going to open my eyes, and she'll be standing over me with a creepy as fuck look in her eyes or something." I almost choked on a bite of food when he said that. On top of being a man whore, Trevor was also as dramatic as Savannah, which was really saying something. "You laugh now, but when this woman is arrested driving across state lines, wearing my head as a hat and a Trevor skin suit, you won't be thinking it's so funny." We both finished eating and paid our bill. We even got a small wave from Emmy on our way out.

Progress.

"YOU WEREN'T KIDDING, this place is a hell hole," Trevor offered as we walked into my apartment. "Cardboard boxes as a dining room table," he deadpanned. "Classy. I see you really made this place your own."

I tossed my keys on the kitchen counter and grabbed a bottle of water from the fridge. "Hey, you don't like it, you can always stay at a motel."

"Couldn't be any worse than this," he muttered under his breath as he looked around.

"Look, it isn't much, but it's a place to crash. I have to get to work, but we can go out for a few beers later tonight. There's a live band playing at Colt's."

"Sounds good to me."

I spent the rest of the day feeling a little less weighted down than I had in a really long time. My buddy was in town for an undetermined amount of time, and it looked like Emmy and I were making finally making some strides—small as they were—toward at least getting a friendship started again. All in all, it was starting out to be a pretty damn good day.

CHAPTER FOURTEEN

EMERSON

"WILL THIS DAY EVER END?" I asked looking up at the black sky. Even the twinkle of the stars wasn't enough to pull me out of my mood. I was currently standing in the parking lot outside of the diner, wishing I had telekinetic powers to unlock my car doors. Unfortunately, the power of mind control was not something I was born with. Locking my keys in my car wouldn't normally be such a bad thing, but I'd somehow managed to lock my cell phone in as well.

I had moved from beating on the windows to trying to jimmy the locks. I needed to Macgyver my way out of this situation. Unfortunately, I was completely out of wire hangers, string, and paperclips.

"This is bullshit!" I yelled out at no one. I managed to find a flat piece of metal and was shoving it down between the door and the window in an attempt to pop the lock. I had absolutely no clue what I was doing, but I'd seen it done in movies, so it couldn't have been that hard. *Right?*

"Hands in the air and step away from the car!" I was instantly blinded from my task by a bright spotlight. *Holy shit! I'm being arrested. I'm being arrested! Wait... what the hell am I being arrested for?*

"Emmy?" the booming voice that had just instructed me to put my hands up asked. "Is that you?"

"Uh... yeah," I responded, feeling like a total idiot. "Can I put my hands down now?"

The spotlight went off, but it was too late, the damage was already done. I was pretty certain my retinas were fried.

"Jesus Christ, Emmy. What the hell are you doing out here?"

"Luke?"

Yep, I was right. Totally blind.

"I can't see shit! Was it really necessary to rob me of the gift of sight for the rest of my life?"

I could hear his distinct, gravelly chuckle, and it instantly made me want to throat punch him. "You'll be okay. Just give your eyes a minute to adjust. Now, you going to answer my question or not?"

Seeing as it had already been the longest day in the history of the world, and had been in desperate need of a bottle of wine *before* I locked my keys in my car, it went without saying that my patience was now non-existent. "I'm dancing a freaking jig, Luke. What the hell does it look like I'm doing?"

"It looks like you're breaking into a car."

"Seriously? If I was going to break into a car, you think I'd pick this piece of crap? This is *my* car. I locked myself out." I turned away and went back to beating the windows with my fists of fury.

"Why didn't you just call someone to help?"

"My phone's in the car," I mumbled under my breath. The last thing I needed was to give him more of a reason to tease me. I already hated him a little bit for laughing in the first place. Adding assault charges to my night by kicking a deputy's ass was *not* something I needed.

"What was that?"

"My phone is in the car!" I admitted on a loud yelp. "There, happy now?"

Luke threw his head back in a roar of laughter.

"I'm *so* glad I could give you a chuckle, asshole. What are you doing here anyway?"

"Mrs. Gillman across the street called and reported seeing someone trying to steal a car," he replied when he was finally able to speak without busting a gut.

I threw my hands in the air in frustration. "Oh come on! Mrs. Gillman can't see *anything*. The woman's been blind since the Nixon administration. You know this."

Luke raised his hands palm side up. "Just doing my job, Emmy."

"Fine," I grumbled. "Well since you're here, can you at least help me pop the lock so I can get home? I'm freaking exhausted."

He walked over to me, and my body immediately responded to his closeness. My breathing sped up like I'd just run a mile at a full sprint, and goose bumps spread across my skin. I wanted to contribute the flutter low in my belly to hunger pains but I knew what it really was. It was lust. And it was inconvenient as hell.

Stupid freaking hormones!

Everything about Luke made my skin tingle, and I hated myself for still being so affected by him. "I'm a cop, not a criminal, Emmy. I don't have the first damn clue how to *pop a lock*," he replied, humor dripping from his words.

I dropped my head onto the roof of the car and started banging it lightly. Luke's massive hand came between my forehead and the cold metal, creating a soft barrier. "Come on now, we don't want to add a concussion on top of everything else you're dealing with tonight. I'll take you home."

"What about my car?" I asked as he dragged me toward his sheriff-issued SUV.

"I'll have a locksmith here in the morning, don't worry about it. I don't think you're really at risk of someone stealing that thing."

Jerking my arm out of his grasp, I turned on him with my hands propped on my hips. "Hey, that car might be a piece of shit, but it's *my* piece of shit. You're not allowed to talk about it like that, only I am."

He looked at me like I'd just grown a horn from my forehead. "You realize you're making absolutely no sense right now, don't you?"

I rubbed the heels of my palms into my eyes. "I'm deliriously tired at the moment," I groaned.

He started pulling me toward his car again. "Let's get you home then." We got into the SUV and he slowly pulled out of the parking lot. "Where to?" I gave him directions to my house then rested my head against the cool glass of the passenger side window.

I was just starting to doze off when Luke's voice broke through the haze of sleep. "I'm sorry about your Grams, Emmy. I know how much you loved her."

A ball of fire formed in my chest, burning and suffocating, pushing that pain to the forefront of my mind once again. "Thank you," I whispered. I could tell he was struggling with what to say next, but I was just too tired to strike up conversation on my own.

"So did you get your degree in psychology like you always talked about?"

And the hits just keep on coming.

"No. Some... stuff happened." *Life happened.* "Grams got sick so I had to take over the diner to keep it running. It was one thing after another, and I just never got the chance to finish it."

"Jesus," he whispered more to himself than to me. "I didn't know. God, I'm so sorry."

Sharing a space with Luke without the buffer of our friends was difficult enough. I couldn't handle his pity as well. "It's in the past," I mumbled. "No reason to dwell on it now."

Maybe it was exhaustion. Or maybe it was just the stress of the past several weeks crashing down on me all at once, but whatever the reason, my next words poured past my lips of their own accord.

"You really never read a single email I sent, did you?" I don't know what possessed me in that moment, and demanded I ask him that. I already knew what he was going to say, and hearing him reconfirm his reasons was going to *kill*. "You know what, don't answer that. I really don't want to know." I went back to staring out the window. Watching Luke shift uncomfortably in his seat was just too much for me handle.

How much pain could a person's heart take before it finally shattered into pieces?

Minutes later, Luke pulled into my driveway, and just as I reached for the door handle, he spoke.

"I couldn't, Emmy." He said it so quietly I almost missed it.

"Luke, don't—"

"I knew if I heard your voice or read any of your emails, I wouldn't be able to let you go." The tears came in full force with his declaration. God, I was so sick of crying. I buried my head in my hands and let them fall silently as he continued. "Back then, I thought I was doing what was best for you... Emmy, please look at me." He put his finger under my chin and lifted my face to his. "I'm so sorry, baby girl. I'd give anything to take away the pain I caused you. Just tell me what to do and I'll do it." He leaned in closer to me as he whispered, "Please, just let me fix this. Let me fix us."

Parting my lips on a sharp inhale was apparently all the

invitation he needed. Before I knew what was happening, Luke had my seatbelt unbuckled and pulled me into his lap. The instant his lips met mine I was lost. It wasn't the slow burn type of kiss. It was vicious and desperate. It was full of undeniable hunger. The need inside both of us had clawed its way to the surface, and we kissed as if our lives depended on it. The feel of his hands on me was completely intoxicating. When he slid his finger beneath my shirt, along the waistband of my shorts, an uncontrollable chill went through my whole body. He feasted on my lips like a man devouring his last meal, creating a simmer in my blood that I could quickly become addicted to.

The few brain cells I had left were screaming at me to stop, that I shouldn't be doing this, but when Luke trailed his lips down my neck and along my collarbone, all rational thought escaped me. I let out a low moan from deep in my throat. Grabbing a hold on his silky black hair, I yanked his mouth to mine and dove back into that kiss. "God, I've missed you so much, baby girl," he said against my lips. I'd missed him too... so damn much. "I never should have left you the way I did."

At his words, memories of the last night I saw him came rushing back to me with the impact of a car smashing into a wall. Allison down on her knees. Luke's voice raspy with passion. It was like a bucket of ice water being poured over me. I pulled back and scrambled across the seat for my door. "Emmy, wait." Luke grabbed me by my waist and hauled me back into his chest.

"Please... Luke, I-I can't do this. It was a mistake." I was pulling against him with all my strength but it was pointless. The guy had more muscle than I originally thought. I knew this as a fact seeing as I just had my hands on almost every part of his body. I could still feel the heat in my palms from touching him.

"I'm sorry. Emmy, I'm sorry. Please just stop fighting for a second, okay? Just let me talk to you." His quietly spoken plea and the desperation in his voice caused the fight to drain right out of me. I slumped back into his chest and waited to hear what he had to say next, mindful to prepare myself for another blow.

"I got carried away," he continued, taking another painful slice right out of me. "I shouldn't have kissed you like that, and I apologize. But I'm not going to let you run away from me every time things get difficult. I promise I won't do anything to make you uncomfortable, but you've got to promise to quit running."

Sucking in some much needed air, I nodded my head. "Okay," I relented on a whisper.

"Okay?" When I heard the surprise in his voice, I knew he had expected an argument. I was just too damn tired.

"Yeah. I said okay. I'll quit running, but you can't touch me like this, Luke." I waved my hands in the direction of where his arms were wrapped around me. "You can't act like it hasn't been eight years since we've seen each other. I don't like how familiar this feels."

He nodded against my hair as he removed his arms from around me, but he moved so slowly it felt like it took an eternity, as though he were trying to drag out the touch for as long as humanly possible, until he was satisfied. I turned to look at him when he spoke. "All right, I can do that. But I need you to understand one thing."

I wasn't sure I could handle much else but that statement had peaked my curiosity. "What?"

"I came back because I had to. I've regretted leaving you for eight years, and I had to come back and see if there was any chance you could forgive me."

I wanted to melt back into him when he said that. But for my own self-preservation, I couldn't. "I can't promise you anything, Luke. I don't know if you and I can ever get back to where we were before."

He ran his fingers lightly down my cheek. "I've got to try, Emmy. Losing you was the worst thing that's ever happened to me. I've at least got to try to earn your forgiveness."

Grabbing hold of his wrist, I pulled his hand away. "I have to go. I'll see you tomorrow." I climbed out and made my way to my front door on wobbly legs, knowing, without a doubt, that I was about to encounter another night without any sleep.

WHEN I CLIMBED out of bed the next morning, my car was parked in the driveway with a note stuck to the windshield.

Emmy,
I'm not giving up. I'll find a way to earn your trust again.
P.S. This car really is a piece of shit.
Yours... ALWAYS,
Luke.

CHAPTER FIFTEEN

LUKE

IT WAS LATE AT NIGHT, *the sky completely black and starless thanks to the earlier thunderstorms that had passed through town. I followed the familiar path between the houses without having to pay attention to where I was going. It was a route I knew by heart, this walk being second nature to me after so many years.*

The window slid open with ease, and I hefted myself up and over the ledge without making a single sound. I could see the form of her body beneath the frilly light blue and yellow comforter, and hear the faint chuffing of her barely-there snores. That noise was all I needed in order to calm the war raging inside of me. My heart rate slowed, and the trembling in my palms lessened as I got closer.

"Baby girl," I whispered.

The snoring sputtered to a stop, and her long arms stretched above her head. "Luke?" Emmy asked on a yawn.

"Yeah."

I watched in the shadows as she sat up and reached to the lamp on her bedside table. A moment later the room filled with a dim, golden light just before she sucked in a startled gasp.

"Oh my god," she whispered, tears welling in her pretty stormy blue eyes while she took in my battered and bruised face. *"What... Did he do this to you?"* My bottom lip twitched in a grin at the sound of the venom in her sugar sweet voice. The grin reopened the cut my father had given me an hour earlier, and I winced at the sudden sting.

"Crap," she hissed, jumping up from the bed. *"Don't smile. Or talk. Just... hold on. You're bleeding."*

Emmy quickly padded across to her desk, and pulled open the bottom drawer. So many times through the years I'd snuck through her window after my father had a go at me, that she'd started stashing first aide supplies in her bedroom.

Finding the alcohol swabs and bandages she needed, Emmy took my hand and pulled me toward the bed, forcing me to sit where she'd just been sleeping.

"Tell me what happened." It was a command. It wasn't a question of whether or not I wanted to talk about it. Emmy wasn't giving me the choice. It was as simple as that. She'd known me for ten years, since I was a scrawny six-year-old boy, so she knew that holding what had happened tonight in would only fester and grow, until I eventually exploded.

"Tonight was different," I admitted in a quiet voice.

Momentarily shifting her gaze from dabbing the cuts on my cheekbone and lip, she stared into my eyes and hesitantly said, *"I know. I don't think it's ever been this bad before."* Worry creased her pretty face as she all but begged, *"Luke, you have to tell somebody. The police or something. You can't keep letting your dad hit you like this—"*

I lifted my hand and put it over her mouth to stop her. *"It's not going to happen anymore,"* I told her in a hard tone.

"You can't know that."

"I can. I know it won't because tonight... I hit back. And I beat the shit out of him, Emmy."

Her eyes bugged out for a split second before a huge, beaming smile spread across her face. "You did?" We continued to speak in whispers so her Grams wouldn't hear.

"I did. And I'll do it again and again if I have to."

Taking her bottom lip between her front teeth, she bit down like she was trying to suppress the grin that had already taken over her face. "How bad is it that I want to tell you I'm so proud of you right now?"

A chuckle worked its way up from my chest. I didn't think I'd be capable of laughing or smiling after the scene that had gone down earlier, but just being around my beautiful Emmy made everything better. "Not bad at all."

She pounced, pulling me into a hug so tight it nearly cut off my air supply. I held her against me, caressing her back as something started to change.

When I pulled back the entire room was different. The light had flickered out, bathing everything in darkness. My gaze landed on Emmy and I noticed her appearance had altered. Her hair was longer. Her face was more mature, like she'd aged a few years in the blink of an eye. Her body was fuller, curvier than it had just been.

"Emmy?" I croaked. "What's going on?"

"I feel like I'm losing a part of me, Luke. I'm going to miss you so much."

A sense of déjà vu took hold of me, and I found my mouth opening to respond without thinking. "I'm going to miss you too, baby girl. More than you know. But you aren't losing me. You'll never lose me. I promise."

This had all happened before. This whole conversation, but for some reason I was reliving it.

I knew exactly what was going to happen next, and my entire body coiled in anticipation.

Emmy's tongue snaked out, running across my bottom lip,

and I lost complete control. Kissing her was better than every dream, every fantasy I could ever imagine. She tasted like the sweetest thing to ever pass my lips.

Then she rolled to her back, holding on to take me with her, and I was ready. So. Goddamn. Ready. But something took over, refusing to let me act.

I ripped my mouth from hers and stared into those stormy blues.

Wrapping her arms and legs around me, she whispered, "Please, Luke," with so much need and desperation I felt it to my bones.

"Emmy, we can't. You've never..." I trailed off at the look of determination on her face. "Emmy, honey, you deserve so much better than me. Your first time should be with somebody you love."

"I do love you, Luke. I always have." My chest grew tight. My heart swelled so goddamn big at hearing her say she loved me, I wasn't sure how to handle the amazing pain. "Please, Luke. I need you."

My cock grew hard as stone. This was what I'd wanted for so fucking long. I watched her face as my hands removed the clothing between us. I was pressing against her slick entrance, about to drive myself into bliss, when suddenly...

The alarm beside my bed began blaring.

I shot up, my chest covered in sweat, my dick standing tall and throbbing behind my boxer briefs.

"*Christ*," I grunted, dragging my hands across my tired face. Being back in Cloverleaf was seriously starting to screw with my head. Each night, I dreamed of Emmy. Memories of the past came flooding into my unconscious mind, twisting and melding themselves together. Each dream started with a different memory of my childhood, but they all ended with the same one.

That night had been the most perfect night of my life. No

woman before or after had lived up to my amazing, innocent Emmy. If I could go back in time and change what happened afterward I would do it, without hesitation. I'd give my life for a chance to do it all over.

A sudden pounding on my bedroom door yanked me from my thoughts. "Yo!" Trevor hollered from the other side. "Time to rise and shine, sweet cheeks! You got bacon in the fridge that isn't gonna cook itself, and I'm fucking starving!"

Son of a bitch. This was going to be a long fucking day."

CHAPTER SIXTEEN

EMERSON

THE NEXT FEW days had been a whirlwind. I saw Luke a few times. He tried his best to be a perfect gentleman, but I couldn't stop replaying that kiss. Just thinking about it made me burn from the inside out. I ached for him in ways I shouldn't. The memory of that kiss was driving me insane, but I couldn't talk to anyone about it. Reminding myself of how badly Luke had hurt me wasn't enough to get the mental pictures out of my head. I was terrified and exhilarated all at the same time. Allowing Luke back in could potentially bring my already shaky world down around me. I just had to keep reminding myself of that.

With everything that was going on in my head, it was a wonder I hadn't forgotten what day it was. When I went into my kitchen to put on a pot of coffee, I noticed the date circled on the calendar. Seeing that helped to ground me a little. With an ache deep inside, I dragged myself through my morning routine and headed out the door. I stopped off at the florist like I usually did every year on this day before making my way to my destination.

The walk up that hill was as sad as it had always been. What I wouldn't have given to never have to do this. I pulled the dead flowers out of the vase and replaced them with the new ones. Then I took a seat on the fresh cut grass and brushed the dirt off of the grave marker in front of me.

WHEN I PULLED up in my driveway hours later, I was emotionally drained, and exhausted from crying. All I wanted to do was crawl back into bed until the day was over.

Brett and Lizzy were sitting on my front porch when I walked up. "You two on Emmy-watch this year?" I asked trying to keep it light even though I was numb inside.

"Don't think of it like that," Brett replied as he stood and pulled me into a hug.

"We just want to be here for you. That's all." Lizzy took my keys and unlocked my door for me. "How are you?"

Rubbing at my temples, I closed my eyes as they led the way to the kitchen and said, "I'm alright. I just hate this day. I wish I could sleep through it every year."

"We're all here for you, honey," Brett replied as he released me and moved over to one of my cabinets.

"I know. And I can't begin to tell y'all how much I appreciate it."

Pulling out one of my kitchen chairs, I plopped down and rested my elbows on the table, the emotions of the day weighing so heavy I could no longer stand. Lizzy came and sat down in front of me. "You know Savannah would be here if she could get off work."

"I know." I loved Savannah so much, but part of me was kind of glad she wasn't here. Our bond was so strong that it would have just been the two of us hugging and crying all day long. At least with Lizzy and Brett, I stood a chance of stepping out of my sorrows for at least a little while.

"What's your poison today, love?" Brett asked. "I'm just going to Irish your coffee up a little bit."

That actually got a laugh out of me. "Bourbon will work just fine."

"That's my girl." He gave me a little wink as he doctored up my coffee. It was just what I needed.

We sat in my kitchen drinking coffee—mine spiked with a healthy dose of booze—talking about nothing in particular, but I could tell by the expression on Brett's face that he had something on his mind. "What's up, Brett?"

"Huh? Nothing…" I couldn't stand it that everyone felt the need to walk on eggshells around me when this day rolled around. I was hurting, but I wasn't so fragile that I'd break. I'd come a very long way over the years. I was so much stronger than I used to be.

I reached over and placed my hand over his. "Just tell me. I know something's bothering you."

He released a sigh before answering. "Are you planning on telling him?"

I ran my hands through my hair trying to figure out what I should do. "I don't know," I said, releasing a huff of air. "Y'all tell me what to do. I'm tired of making these decisions on my own."

Lizzy looked at me sympathetically, which was almost as bad as pity. "You know we can't do that. You have to decide if you want him to know now that he's back, or not."

I rubbed my aching temples and took the coward's way out… avoidance. "Can we not talk about this? I'm not trying to be rude, but I just can't handle this today."

I laid my head on the table in front of me as Brett rubbed my hair. "I'm sorry I brought it up. And you aren't being rude for not wanting to discuss this, today of all days."

Looking back up at him, I saw the regret written on his face.

"Don't be sorry, Brett. I'm the one who asked you to tell me what you're thinking."

"I still shouldn't have."

I couldn't let him beat himself up for speaking his mind. "Stop. I'm not upset, I promise." He smiled at me, the relief evident in his expression. "So what's the plan for tonight?" On this day every year, my friends always made plans for the evening. Whether we went out or stayed in, we did something and we did it together. They were all there and all worked to keep my mind off of the past. The only difference was that, this year, Luke would be joining us.

I didn't want him to think we were intentionally leaving him out. It would have led to him ask questions I didn't want to answer. To make sure things didn't get too awkward, I also invited Trevor to join us as well.

"Three words," Lizzy said, excitedly. "Daryl. Rick. Zombies!"

I couldn't contain my squeal. I went totally girly and started bouncing in my seat. *"The Walking Dead* marathon?"

"Ding, ding, ding."

"*Yay!*" Good friends and a marathon of my favorite show were all I was going to need to make it through this day.

"OH!" came the collective gasp from the crowd.

"Jesus, I didn't know this show was so graphic," Luke grunted as we watched a scene where a particularly large zombie started ripping into a screaming woman's intestines.

"I know. It's great isn't it?" I squeaked excitedly.

"How have I never seen this show?" That question came from Trevor who was sitting on the couch with his elbows on his knees, absolutely captivated by what was happening on the screen.

"The only answer is that you're a total loser," Lizzy answered with a smirk. I'd noticed the two of them subtly flirting throughout the night. Small things, like throwing playful insults at each other like two eight year olds, but it was still a lot fun to watch.

I was sitting between Luke and Jeremy on the couch, thoroughly enjoying the evening. "Andrea's kind of hot," Luke said to me with a grin. I punched him in the arm and let out a laugh.

"Yeah, if you consider a woman with a toxic va-jay-jay hot," Savannah said seriously. I had to hand it to her and Brett, the two of them were working pretty hard at being polite to Luke. It definitely helped make this day even easier.

"Toxic va-jay-jay?" he sputtered in confusion.

"Yeah, you saw how Shane went nutso because Lori and Rick had to kill him."

"Yeah..."

"And now Andrea is banging the Governor and he's clearly off his rocker."

"Uh huh..."

"And now Rick's seeing the ghost of his wife everywhere he turns. You see the pattern?"

"Not really."

"Well, Savannah and I have this theory. Lori screwed both Rick and Shane, and Andrea screwed Shane and the Governor. Savannah and I think that all three went crazy from toxic va-jay-jay poisoning."

"Huh," he said, as if giving that some thought. "Strangely, that makes perfect sense."

"Told ya." I smiled up at him when I caught a glimpse of Savannah from the corner of my eye. She was watching our exchange so closely I could feel the heat from her gaze piercing my skin.

"I don't give a shit," Trevor stated seriously, eyes still glued to the TV. "I'd rather go crazy from having sex than get my intestines ripped out by some dude with half his face rotted off."

"Why am I not surprised?" Luke rolled his eyes at Trevor. "I think some of those women you've been with already caused brain rot."

Trevor threw a beer cap at Luke's head. "Don't hate just because you haven't gotten any in years."

Luke's spine instantly stiffened, and a small gasp burst past my lips at Trevor's statement. It seemed like everyone except Trevor was suddenly on red alert. All conversation came to a halt and every person's eyes darted to Luke and me.

"What? What'd I say?" Poor Trevor was totally clueless.

I gave him a polite smile and responded "Nothing. It's all good." I stood from the couch and made my way to the kitchen. "I'm getting another beer. Anybody need a refill?" I didn't wait around for anyone to respond before booking it to the kitchen.

Savannah came in a minute later to find me with my palms on the island and my head hung down. "You okay, honey?"

I inhaled deeply and let it out just as slowly. "Yeah... No.... God, I don't know." I took a few more deep, cleansing breaths.

"How about now?" she asked. She stood there calmly while I tried to pull my shit together.

"Yeah. I think I'm good now."

She walked over to stand beside me and leaned into me. "I'm not going to give you a hard time. I just want to make sure you know what you're doing."

That was her subtle way of mentioning how Luke and I were acting towards each other. The fact that she wasn't going to lay into me and tell me I was making a huge mistake was a massive relief. "I'm not going to lie, Savvy. I really don't have a fucking clue what I'm doing." We both laughed at that. "But I'm just taking things one day at a time and trying to do what makes me happy."

She wrapped me in a tight hug. "That's all I want. For you to be happy. If taking it one day at a time to see how things play out makes you happy, then I'll back you... every step of the way."

We headed back into the living room, fresh beers in hand, just in time to hear Jeremy yell "Shots! That zombie went for the jugular. That's a shot!"

The only thing better than watching *The Walking Dead* was turning it into a drinking game. Whenever a zombie went straight for the throat, everybody had to do a shot.

After the day I had, I was glad—and slightly surprised—to be having such a great night. I grabbed the shot glass Stacia held up for me and downed it with a smile.

CHAPTER SEVENTEEN

EMERSON

EVERYONE STARTED to file out after we watched Andrea bite the bullet. Trevor was still having trouble coping with the fact that Merle didn't make it. Standing at my front door, he looked at me with a hangdog expression. "I just don't understand. Why did it have to be Merle?"

Reaching up, I patted him on the head. "It's just a TV show, Trev. Don't get so emotionally invested."

"It should have been Glenn. That guy's been acting like a little bitch ever since he got back from Woodbury. It should have been him."

I pulled him into a hug and tried to stifle my laughter. "Tell you what. Next marathon night we'll watch *New Girl*. It's funny as hell and it'll pull you out of your zombie-induced depression."

He was still mumbling about how unfair it was as he made his way to his car. Closing the door, I turned around to find Luke picking up the empty beer bottles scattered around my living room. "Your friend has issues," I said as I joined the cleanup.

"That's an understatement."

"You really don't have to help clean. I planned on getting to it in the morning."

He lifted his shoulder in a slight shrug. "It's no big deal." Luke finished picking up in the living room, and I headed to the kitchen to start in there. He joined me a few minutes later. Resting his hip against the island, he watched me for several seconds as I cleaned before saying, "This was a lot of fun."

I looked up from where I was wiping down the counter and smiled genuinely. "Yeah, it really was."

He just stood there, looking deep in thought as he flipped a beer cap between his thumb and index finger over and over. "I just want to thank you. You know... for inviting me and Trevor."

Placing the dishrag on the counter, I faced Luke full on, and folded my arms over my chest. "Well, we're trying to be civil toward each other, right?" A smile spread across my face as I continued, "And besides, Trevor's a hot mess. It's always fun to have someone like that around."

Luke let out a small laugh before getting serious again. "I know Brett and Savannah still have issues with me, but it was nice being able to be here with no drama."

The need to defend them dominated everything else. "They're just protective of me. I'm sure they'll eventually get over it. You shouldn't take it personally."

"It's definitely personal, Emmy, but I'm not mad about it. I understand why they look at me the way they do, and honestly, I'm glad you've got people like them at your back. I fucked up, and they're watching to make sure I don't do it again."

Suddenly meeting his eyes was difficult. Dropping my head, I looked at my feet as I said, "They'll come around eventually."

I could sense him moving closer just before I felt his fingertips under my chin, lifting my face, so we were eye to eye. "What about you, Emmy? Have you come around?"

As I looked into those green eyes, I understood just how

deep the meaning behind that question ran, and I couldn't allow myself to sink into those depths with him.

"I can try and give you my friendship, Luke, but that's all I've got. And even then, I'm still struggling."

My heartbeat stalled as those deep green emeralds scanned every inch of my face just before a smile took over, taking Luke from handsome to downright gorgeous in the blink of and eye. "That's good enough," he said as he started for the door. I'd just released my breath when he added, "For now." The front door closed with a resounding click that echoed through my brain like a gunshot.

Well shit. That's not good.

LUKE

"YOU'RE KIDDING RIGHT?" Trevor asked in disbelief. "You hate clubs. The few times I dragged your ass to one, you stood up against the wall looking like someone pissed in your corn flakes."

I took off my gun belt and sat it on the bed before heading to my closet. Emmy and the rest of the girls had decided they wanted to go dancing that night, and I wasn't missing out on an opportunity to spend time with the woman who had plagued my thoughts every moment of the past eight years. I yanked a black button-down off the hanger in my closet and tossed it on the bed. "Well, this is what everyone decided they wanted to do. It's either go to a club or sit in this shitty apartment all night."

"You don't even dance."

I finished discarding my uniform and quickly redressed in the black shirt and a pair of well worn jeans. I only had twenty minutes to finish getting ready before I had to meet everyone in the parking lot of Virgie May's. "Who said I had to dance? I'm just going to hang out and have a few beers. It's not a big deal, Trev."

He looked skeptical. "Uh huh."

I rolled my eyes and asked, "You coming or not?"

"Oh, I'm coming all right. I've never seen you trip over yourself for a piece of ass before. Emmy's got you in knots, and I'm not gonna miss a second of this."

I quickly turned around and shoved my finger in Trevor's face, red coating my vision. "Refer to Emmy as a piece of ass one more time, and I'll break my foot off in yours. We clear?"

"Whoa." Trevor held up his hands and took a step back with an uncomfortable laugh. "Crystal clear, brother." He stood silently, examining like a bug under a magnifying glass before speaking again. "What happened with you two? I know there's a story there, so don't bother denying it."

Dropping my head to look up at the ceiling, I raked my hands through my hair. The knot that had been residing in my gut for so damn long was finally starting to grow unbearable. I wasn't sure how much longer I could handle carrying it around with me.

I really didn't want to get into mine and Emmy's past, but I knew the likelihood of Trevor being put off again was slim to none. "I moved down the street from Emmy when I was about six. She was my best friend all my life until I joined the Corps."

"So what happened? She wasn't cool with you enlisting or something?"

Giving up the hope of being able to cliff notes what had happened, I dropped down on the edge of my bed and continued. "Nah, she eventually got used to the idea. I mean, she wasn't thrilled at first, but she always supported my decisions." He just stood there, waiting for me to go on. Pulling in a deep breath, I spoke for the first time about the worst decision I'd ever made. "A few days before I left, we ended up sleeping together. I freaked out and did something really fucking stupid to try and push her away."

"What'd you do?" Leave it to Trevor to ask the questions I didn't want to answer.

"I picked up a chick from a party... I knew Emmy and this girl hated each other, that's why I chose her. I was leaving for basic the next day, and I wasn't answering any of Emmy's calls. I knew she'd come looking for me before I took off, so I took the girl home and Emmy walked in on us."

I sat there, letting Trevor process what I just told him while my mind took me back to that night. For the past eight years I'd hated myself. I couldn't even look in the mirror without snarling at the bastard standing in front of me. That self-loathing hadn't gotten any better as time passed.

"What the fuck, man?" he finally snapped after several very tense seconds. "That's just twisted. Why the hell would you do something like that? From what I've seen, Emmy's fucking awesome."

I let out a groan before answering. "I know... *Fuck*! I know, all right. I said it was stupid. I was twenty years old and freaking the hell out. It was a mistake."

"Dude, no wonder she's been pissed at you for so long. Shit," he hissed, running a hand through his hair. "She's a better person than I am. Someone pulled shit like that, they'd be dead to me. You're lucky she's even talking to you now."

I wanted to be pissed at what he was saying, but every part of me knew he was right. "Thanks for stating the obvious, man. Now you know the story. Can we drop fucking drop it?"

"After a curt nod from him, Trevor and I headed out of the apartment to meet everybody. "Look," I started, stopping at my truck. "I know what I did was messed up, but I'm back now, and

I'm trying to fix it. That's all I got. It's the only thing I know to do."

Trevor slapped me on the back before heading around the passenger side. "For your sake, I hope you can. Emmy's cool as shit. Hell, she's the type of girl that would make even *me* consider a serious relationship."

Even though I knew it was irrational, my muscles strung tight. "You try, and I'll break every bone in your body."

His head fell back on a burst of laughter as he climbed into the truck. Damn, but that dude never took anything seriously.

CHAPTER EIGHTEEN

EMERSON

"I DON'T CARE how much you love Taylor Swift. If you request one more damn song, I'm going to punch you in the ovary." I felt like me ears were bleeding. One more minute of her voice and I was going to lose my freaking mind.

"Oh, come on!" Savannah whined. "I haven't even heard "I Knew You Were Trouble" yet!"

"And you won't if you're smart. The only thing worse than listening to her is listening to *you* sing along to every one of her songs. It's like two cats being shoved in a sack, beaten with sticks, and then run over." I wasn't intentionally trying to hurt Savannah's feelings; she really *was* that awful.

"Geez, Emmy, talk about a shot to the heart."

Trevor cut in then. "Have you heard yourself sing, *cheri*? You're hot and all, but damn. It's...I can't even...It's just...really fucking bad." The fact that he couldn't even form a coherent sentence to describe the level of awful that was Savannah's singing said it all.

Everyone at the table laughed as Savannah grumbled about how much we all sucked. The night had been amazing so far. I could tell that Brett wasn't one hundred percent on board with

Luke being back in the fold, but he was still able to act somewhat pleasant. Even though all of the guys refused to dance, everyone was enjoying themselves. When "I'm Sexy and I Know It" came over the speakers, Stacia and Lizzy both squealed and pulled Savannah and me out onto the dance floor.

I was having so much fun there was no way I was going to let the pain caused by my four-inch platform heels keep me down, even if I wouldn't be able to walk for a couple of days afterward.

When I spun around, the sight in front of me nearly had me toppling off of those heels. Standing next to Luke was one of the prettiest women I'd ever seen. Her shiny blonde hair hung down her back in waves that I couldn't have pulled off with all the product in the world. The tiny black dress she was wearing would have looked trashy on someone else—say, me—but on her, it looked fantastic. Even *I* was mesmerized by her killer legs. How was it possible for a person to have legs that damn long? I instantly hated the chick. I was a hot, sweaty mess from dancing and could barely walk in my ridiculous shoes, and she looked like a freaking rock star.

Luke's head fell back with bark of laughter at something she whispered in his ear and my chest constricted violently at the sound. Illogical jealousy flooded my system at seeing him with another woman.

Why couldn't I just get over him?

My bright mood deteriorated and when I turned back, I caught Savannah's gaze. Her brows furrowed when she saw the distress written all over my face. Her eyes travelled over to where I'd been looking and the furrow disappeared, quickly replaced with sympathy and understanding.

She pointed over to the bar and I didn't hesitate. I pushed my way through the crowded dance floor and plopped down on one of the vacant stools. My feet were throbbing and I was suddenly miserable. Once she was next to me, she scowled and started right in. "No, Emmy. *Do not* do this."

"Do what?" Denial and feigning ignorance were pointless when it came to Savannah, but that didn't stop me from trying.

"Don't give me that. You know exactly what I'm talking about." Her attention travelled back over to the table where Luke was sitting with Club Barbie. I followed her gaze, and felt that telltale pain flair up again. Tears started to burn the backs of my eyes, and I blinked fast to keep them at bay. Savannah caught me, and the pitying look she gave me only made things worse. "Damn it," she whispered. "I knew this was going to happen."

God, I was so pathetic. "What the hell is wrong with me, Savvy? It's like I'm a fucking glutton for punishment. I don't *want* to want him, so why can't I just stop?"

She reached over and wiped away the few stray tears that had escaped. "I don't know what to say. I wish I had the answers, but I don't. All I know is if you keep going like this, you're going to end up exactly where you were before. You have to make a choice, Emmy. You can either be friends with Luke, and find a way to handle seeing him with other women, or you can cut the strings. Just accept that a friendship with him isn't possible and finally let him go once and for all."

Taking a several deep breaths, I worked to calm the jumble of emotions raging and keep any more tears from falling. "You're right. I know you are but—*shit*, I didn't think it would be this hard."

Reaching up, Savvy ran her hands along my hair soothingly, "I know you don't want to hear this, but maybe it's time for you to start moving on."

"What do you mean?"

"You haven't dated since... Well, you haven't dated in a really long time. Maybe it's time to put yourself out there again.

You're only twenty-six. You deserve to find a guy who worships the ground you walk on. Preferably one you don't have such a tangled history with."

The idea of starting a relationship hadn't appealed to me in a very long time. My friends all knew why, so they never really push, but considering Luke was back in town, maybe it was time. The problem was I didn't have the first clue where to start. I was a twenty-six-year-old woman who had no idea how to even begin putting myself out there. None of my past experiences with men made me want to try again. There were so many things I had to take into consideration before I decided if I was ready. But the main thing was, I had to be sure that I was considering dating again for the *right* reasons.

I didn't want to open myself up to the possibility of another man just because of Luke's return. That wouldn't be fair to me or the other person. I had to make certain my head was in the right place.

I voiced my concerns to Savannah, but I got the impression that she'd stopped paying attention. "Well, love. Looks like you're going to have to figure that out sooner rather than later."

"Why do you say that?" I asked.

"Because you've got one tall, dark and handsome coming your way right this second. I'll leave you two alone."

I grabbed for her arm in a panic. Was I ready for this? "Don't you dare, you bitch," I whisper-yelled.

She hissed back, "It's for your own good."

"You walk away and I swear, you better sleep with one eye open."

She turned and looked over her shoulder and shouted at nobody, "What's that, Lizzy? Yeah, I'll be right there." Then she took off.

She was so dead the next time I got my hands on her.

"Hi," a voice came from behind me before I had a chance to

escape. When I spun around, I was shocked to see that Savannah hit the nail on the head. This guy was most definitely tall, dark and *extremely* handsome.

Well hello, I thought to myself. I stared for several more seconds before realizing I was gawking like a complete moron and hadn't responded back. "Uh... Hi."

Freaking brilliant, Emmy!

I could see the rise and fall of his shoulders as he chuckled. Sparing me any more humility, he held out his hand and introduced himself. "I'm Chase."

"Emerson," I responded, placing my palm in his to shake. There was one thing that immediately stood out from our handshake. Chase's hands were really soft. Like, freakishly soft. It was obvious that he hadn't done a single day of manual labor in his life. His skin was so soft that I started to feel self-conscious about my own hands.

Soft hands aside, the guy had an amazing smile. "It's nice to meet you, Emerson. Can I buy you a drink?"

"Yeah, sure," I replied, giving him my full-watt beam. I might not have been sure if I was ready to jump back into the dating pool again, but that didn't mean I couldn't do a little harmless flirting. And who better to flirt with than a dude who looked like he just stepped off the cover of GQ?

Sitting at the bar talking to Chase, it didn't take long to realize there wasn't a love connection between us. It wasn't because I didn't enjoy talking with him; we just weren't all that compatible. But what our conversation did help me to realize was I'd forgotten just how nice it felt to be the soul focus of a man's attention. I hadn't allowed myself to receive that kind of attention in so long, and I suddenly felt myself craving it. I had no desire to take things any further with Chase, but that didn't mean I wasn't enjoying the hell out of our exchange. I was having too much fun.

We couldn't have been talking for more than a half hour when Luke came stalking up to the bar and pushed his way between Chase and me. "You about ready to go?" he asked in a hard clip. Brows furrowed and eyes dark, it wasn't hard to tell he was angry about something. I just didn't know what that something was.

"Uh... This is Chase." I pointed back and forth waiting for Luke to acknowledge the other man. When he didn't, I glared and turned back to my bar companion. "Chase, the guy who just rudely interrupted us is Luke, an old friend."

Chase tried to be polite and extended his hand to shake. "How you doing, man"

Luke just let out a grunt and turned back to me. "You ready to go or what? Everyone wants to head out."

I leaned around him to apologize to Chase, then grabbed Luke's arm and pulled him away. "What the hell is your problem?" I spat.

"My problem is we're ready to leave, and you're slowing us all down." His hard, aggressive demeanor hadn't changed one bit since the start of our conversation. If anything, he only seemed to be getting angrier.

"Then go, no one's stopping you. I came in my own car."

"You've been drinking." He crossed his arms over his broad chest like he was settling in for a fight.

"I've had half a drink in the past hour. You want to leave? Then leave. I'm not keeping you here. Now, if you'll excuse me, I'm going to go back to Chase."

I barely made it around Luke's massive body when his hand grabbed my elbow and jerked me back around. "You don't even know that guy. No fucking way am I leaving you here alone with him."

That was all it took for me to snap. I got as close to him as I could without touching him, and stood on my tiptoes to be closer to eye level. "Let's get one thing straight right now: you *are not* my dad, my boss, or my man. You want to have a power trip, do it with someone else because I will *not* put up with that bullshit. If you've got an issue with the person I'm talking to, you keep it to yourself because it's none of your damn business. You've been gone for eight years, so let me fill you in on some things. You do not know me. The person I was before you left has been gone for a long time now, so don't make the mistake of acting like you do."

All my little speech seemed to do was infuriate him further. "If you think I'm just going to leave your ass here with some stranger that's probably just trying to get in your pants, think a-fuckin'-gain! I know what that douchebag's after, and I'll break every bone in his goddamned body before I allow him to act on anything in his perverted little mind. Now you've got two choices. You can either leave with the rest of us, nice and quiet, or I can carry your ass out. Either way works for me."

I narrowed my eyes at him, grinning viciously as I threw back, "You sure that little piece you were talking up earlier wouldn't mind you carrying me out of here? She didn't strike me as the type of woman who likes to share." I'd crossed a line I shouldn't have with that statement.

He leaned down so close I could smell the mint and alcohol on his breath. "You jealous, baby girl?"

"Not on your life, asshole. I'm done with this." I shoved past him and started for the table my friends had just vacated.

"Is this you running again?" he asked in a sarcastic tone. "I say a few things you don't like, so you bail?"

That had me stopping in my tracks. "I'm not running, you stupid jerk. You want to go home, so I'm getting my purse. You got a problem with that?" I didn't wait for him to respond before grabbing my purse and heading out the door. Before climbing into my car and shutting the door, I did something extremely immature that I was *not* proud of. "Goodnight, Deputy Dickhead."

And with that, I slammed my car door just as Luke's bark of laughter rang out into the night air.

CHAPTER NINETEEN

LUKE

"HEY, BABY. BUY ME A DRINK?" I unwillingly dragged my gaze away from the dance floor. I would have been perfectly content to watch Emmy dance all night, so I wasn't too thrilled that this chick had just distracted me.

"Sorry. What?"

"I said," she leaned over and shoved her tits in my face as she whispered in my ear, "buy me a drink and maybe I'll make it worth your while."

I threw my head back and laughed. "Is that right?" I asked, still chuckling.

"Oh yeah, honey." I let my eyes travel from her long-ass legs all the way back up to her fake rack. Some guys might be into the whole plastic thing, but I preferred my girl to be natural. There was nothing natural about this chick. Fake blonde hair, fake nails, fake tan, and fake tits. She was hot and all, but I had my eye on the little thing on the dance floor with rich brown hair and gorgeous gray-blue eyes. There wasn't a damn thing fake about Emmy.

"Not tonight, sweetheart." I turned away from her, hoping she'd get the hint. I wasn't that lucky.

Pulling an empty chair so close she was practically in my lap, she sat down and leaned even closer. "Come on, baby, you know you want to."

The sound of her voice was grating. Why did women think it was sexy when they used that whiny baby talk? It made it that much easier to brush her off.

"Woman, what part of *not tonight* makes you think I'm interested in anything you got to offer?" Worrying that Emmy might see this life-sized Barbie practically sitting in my lap, and get the wrong impression made my blood run cold.

When she finally stood up and stomped off in a huff, I caught Trevor laughing at the other end of the table. "You know, you could've helped."

"I could have," he said, still laughing. "But that shit was just too damn funny."

"Oh. So it had nothing to do with the fact that you were too busy following Lizzy around like a dog on a leash all damn night?" I knew I had him there. I'd never seen him so in tune to one woman before.

His laughter cut off immediately. "Fuck off, man." He stood and walked away, and I turned my attention back to the dance floor but Emmy was no longer there.

Shit!

I scanned the whole area but couldn't find her anywhere. I was just about to stand up from my chair and go on a search when I caught sight of Savannah heading back over to the table. "Where's Emmy?" I sounded desperate even to my own ears, but the fact she was no longer in my line of sight set me on edge. Bad shit happened to women every goddamn day.

With a smirk on her face, Savannah pointed her thumb over her shoulder toward the bar, and what I say did absolutely jack shit to sooth my now frantically beating heart. "Over there talking to that fine specimen of man meat."

Anger clouded my vision. Sure enough, Emmy was sitting up at the bar with some tool dressed in a three-piece suit. Who the fuck wore a suit to a bar anyway? "Are you fucking kidding me?" I muttered as Emmy threw her head back with a laugh and ran her hand down the fucker's arm.

Savannah stepped in front of me, blocking my view of Emmy. "What's *your* problem? It's not like you weren't preoccupied over here anyway."

I most definitely wasn't in the mood to deal with her right then. And what she said just confirmed my fear. Emmy saw me with the blonde and got the wrong idea. "It wasn't like that. The bitch just wouldn't take no for an answer."

Why am I defending myself to her?

"Yeah. I'm so sure."

"Look..." I stood and stared Savannah right in the eye. "You don't believe me, that's your deal. I really don't give a shit. But I'm not going to have you running to Emmy and telling her something that isn't true. I had no interest in that woman. I told her to leave and when she didn't, I made sure she got the hint. If you want confirmation, just ask Trevor. He was sitting here the whole time."

A strange expression crossed her face for a split second before she masked it. "I'll be straight with you," she started. It was never a good thing when someone started a sentence like that. "I don't like you."

Yep. Definitely never a good thing.

"Yeah. I kind of got that."

"You've hurt Emmy once, and I'm pretty certain you'll do it again. And when you do, I'll be on your ass like a spider monkey jacked up on Mountain Dew." She took a deep breath then continued. "For some insane reason, she's decided to give your friendship another chance which, I might add, I *totally* disagree with. But I support that girl in everything she does, so until you fuck up again, I guess I'm stuck with you."

"I can feel the love from here, Savannah. Who knew you had so much in your heart?"

She reached out and slapped my arm. "Shut up, ass wipe."

I took that as my cue. "Well, if we've got our bonding out of the way, I have something to take care of. Do me a favor and let everyone know we're leaving." I booked it straight to the bar and shoved my way between Emmy and the fuckwad currently staring at my girl's rack. I ignored the look of shock on her face, too far gone to give a damn if what I did pissed her off. There was another man touching what was mine. She was lucky I hadn't already put my fist through his goddamn face.

"You about ready to go?" I interrupted. I vaguely heard her introduce me to the loser she was with. I didn't want his name, I just wanted to get her the hell away from him. "You ready to go or what? Everyone wants to head out."

She jerked me away from the asshole and started rambling on. The blood rushing in my ears was so loud, I barely heard her ask what my problem was. I was sure I answered her back, but my brain had quit running on all cylinders the minute I saw her with another man. I just about lost my mind when she informed me she was going back to whatever his name was.

"You don't even know that guy. No fucking way am I leaving you here alone with him." That was the wrong thing to say. She lit into me without a second of hesitation, and it wasn't lost on me just how sexy she looked right then as she yelled at me.

I was so turned on I wasn't hearing a damn word she was saying. That was, until she made a comment about me not knowing her any longer.

Alarm bells began blaring in my skull. She thought I didn't know her? Eight goddamn years didn't change the connection we'd had since we were kids. I knew her better than I knew myself.

We continued to spar for another minute or so before I finally had enough. I wasn't going to stand there and fight with her about some guy she didn't even know. "Now you've got two choices. You can either leave with the rest of us, nice and quiet, or I can carry your ass out. Either way works for me." I was really hoping she'd take me up on my offer to carry her. I'd been itching to get my arms around her from the moment I set my eyes on her in Virgie May's after eight long years. That night in my truck, with her lips against mine, and her body pressed tight to my chest only made my need that much stronger.

I could have sworn, when she narrowed her eyes at me in a challenge, I got hard enough to hammer nails. I loved her feisty little attitude. "You sure that little piece you were talking up early wouldn't mind you carrying me out of here? She didn't strike me as the type of woman who likes to share."

Lust and desire started pumping through my blood. "You jealous, baby girl?" That was, by far, the stupidest thing I could have said, but I couldn't help myself. She just looked so sexy standing there, fire flashing in her thundercloud eyes. I pushed her buttons to get a reaction just so I could watch the sparks ignite.

"Not on your life, asshole," she threw at me. "I'm done with this."

That one simple statement snuffed out the desire, leaving fear in its wake.

Not again.

I couldn't lose her now that I was so close to getting her back. "Is this you running again?" I couldn't stand the thought of that. "I say a few things you don't like, so you bail?"

"I'm not running, you stupid jerk. You want to go home, so I'm getting my purse. You got a problem with that?"

Thank Christ.

I followed her all the way out to her car, relieved that she was leaving without talking to that guy again. "Goodnight, Deputy Dickhead," she hollered at me, and I couldn't help myself. I burst out laughing as she slammed her car door, started up, and took off.

I knew she wasn't anywhere near ready to accept that I wanted us to be together, but I was willing to wait. I'd spent the last eight years comparing every woman that crossed my path to Emmy, and every one of them fell short by miles. I'd spent nearly a decade knowing there was no other woman for me. I just hoped I hadn't done too much damage.

CHAPTER TWENTY

EMERSON

WHEN I WALKED out of the kitchen, Luke was sitting at one of the tables, looking over a menu. I didn't know why he bothered. He'd ordered the same thing for breakfast for as long as I could remember. "Lenny, give me a number four for the deputy," I hollered over my shoulder as I made my way to his table.

I put my hands on my hips and stared him down, shooting lasers from my eyes. An apologetic expression enveloped his face when he lifted his gaze to mine. "You still mad at me?"

I propped my hands on my hips and made a face that clearly stated not to mess with me. "You done acting like an asshole?"

He gave me a devilish grin. "That depends. Are you planning on being alone with anymore strange men?"

"Luke." I said his name as a warning. "You've got to stop this."

"Emmy, I—"

I lifted my hand to cut him off and sat down across from him. "I'm serious. I've already told you that all we can be is friends, and I can barely handle that most days. This is a delicate balance, Luke. I need you to appreciate that. You can't go around intimidating guys that talk to me. It's not fair."

"That guy was an asshole, Emmy."

He was unbelievable. "How do you possibly know that?" I cried, throwing my arms out at my sides in frustration.

"What kind of guy wears a three piece suit to a club? Christ, he screamed tool bag from a mile away."

Once again, we were quickly getting off topic. I had to put the conversation back on course. "Luke, if you're going to live here, you have to deal with me talking to other men. I'm going to date, and so are you. If this is going to work, you have to accept that."

It was obvious by the look on his face that he didn't agree with me, but all he offered was an apology. "I'm sorry. I was out of line and I won't do it again. I promise."

He looked so contrite that I couldn't stop myself from reaching over and placing my hand on top of his. The same electric charge that I felt every time our skin made contact shot through me, and I wondered if he felt it too. Then I looked into his eyes and saw that he did.

I started feeling awkward and pulled back. Luckily, the moment was cut short when his cell phone went off. He lifted his finger, indicating he just needed a moment before he answered. "Allen," he said in a strong, authoritative tone. His face dropped as the person on the other end spoke. "Yeah, Mom. I'll be right there." He slid his finger across the screen, ending the call before looking back at me.

"Is everything okay?" He stood up and took his wallet out of his pocket. He started to put a twenty on the table but I stopped him. "Luke, you didn't even eat. You aren't paying for something you didn't get. Why don't I make it to go?"

He looked panicked as he nodded his head, so I rushed to the kitchen and quickly boxed up his breakfast. When I came back out, he was running his hands roughly through his hair.

"Luke, what's going on? Is everything alright with your mom?"

"She had an accident. I have to go." He started for the door, but I couldn't let him leave in his current state.

"Luke!" I called as I ran out the door after him. "Luke, let me drive. Please. You're really shaken up right now." I became even more concerned when he didn't put up a fight. He just tossed me the keys to his truck and headed around the passenger side. "Where are we going?" I asked as I climbed in and started it up.

"The hospital."

Shit.

"Okay." I drove in silence, checking on Luke out of the corner of my eye every few minutes. Anyone who didn't know him would probably think he was fine, but from the way his knee was bouncing up and down quickly, I knew he was freaking the hell out. "What happened?"

He rubbed his hands over his face several times before answering. "I don't know. She just called me and said she had an accident and had to call an ambulance. Since I wasn't on duty, I didn't hear the call come in."

"Maybe that's a good thing... you know, that you weren't at work when it happened." I knew from far too much experience that nothing I was saying would make him feel any better, but I had to try.

"I guess."

He closed himself off at that point, and neither of us spoke another word as we drove the last few miles to the hospital. I pulled into the parking lot, and the truck barely came to a full stop before Luke jumped out and booked it to the doors of the emergency room.

Throwing it into park, I jumped out, hit the locks and ran after him. He was already at the nurse's station when I got to him. "I'm looking for Ilene Allen. She was brought in a few minutes ago." On instinct, I grabbed his hand when I noticed it shaking. He glanced down at our joined fingers and gave them a squeeze before looking back up at me with a smile that didn't quite reach his eyes. I smiled back, trying to make him feel a little better. If that was even possible.

"Mr. Allen, if you'll just have a seat over there, the doctor will be right with you."

The nurse's bored, disinterested tone grated at my nerves. I got that her job could cause desensitization, but there were family members to consider.

I pulled Luke over to the row of chairs lining the window in the mostly empty waiting room. When he rested his elbows on his knees and hung his head I felt utterly helpless. All I could think was that I wished there was something I could say to make him feel better, but I knew there wasn't.

I let my eyes wander around the waiting room, taking in the drab off white walls and bright florescent lighting. I hated everything about hospitals: the smell of the disinfectant, the sounds of beeping monitors, and the hushed murmur of voices in the hallways. It all brought back awful memories that I couldn't stand to remember, but I knew I had to stay for Luke.

His voice pulled me back to reality. "You don't have to stay. I appreciate you driving me, but I'm sure you've got better things to do."

It was my turn to squeeze his hand. "I've got nothing better to do. Besides..." I said with a grin, "...we came in your truck." I was finally able to get a smile out of him.

"Thank you," he whispered. "It means a lot that you're here."

"Of course. We're friends, Luke. This is what friends do."

He leaned back in the chair and stared up at the ceiling for a while. "She was probably fucking drunk again."

I cringed at his words. Everyone in town knew his mom had been an alcoholic when we were growing up. As far as I was concerned back then, she'd let her husband beat up on not just her, but her baby boy as well. Just the sight of her sent my anger through the roof, so once Luke was gone I made it my mission to avoid Ilene Allen as much as possible. I'd see her around town occasionally, but that was all. She never came into the diner, and from what I gathered through the town grapevine, never really left her house that often.

"She still has a drinking problem?"

He let out a heavy sigh. "Yeah. But that's not really surprising, is it?" I wasn't sure what to say to that, so I remained quiet.

We sat there in silence until the doctor came out to talk to Luke. It turned out that Ilene was, in fact, drunk and had taken a tumble down the cement stairs of her back porch. "We did some x-rays and nothing is broken. She's extremely lucky. No concussion, just a gash on her forehead that required stitching. It could have been much worse."

I relaxed a little at the news that she was going to be okay. "Thanks, Doc. Will I be able to take her home today?"

With a sympathetic look, he answered, "I don't see any reason why not. But I need to make you aware of the fact that when your mother was brought in, there was a large quantity of alcohol in her system."

Luke let out a laugh devoid of any humor. "You aren't telling me anything I don't already know, Doc. That woman's been drunk pretty much every day of my life."

The doctor shrank back at Luke's harsh tone. I decided that maybe it was time for me to step in. "Can we go back there and see her?"

That earned me an appreciative smile from the older man, and I could have sworn I heard a growl come from Luke. "Sure, go on back. I'll get the release papers set and you'll be able to leave shortly."

He walked off, and Luke and I started down the hall to where his mom was. "I don't like that guy," he stated firmly but quietly as we walked.

"You talked to him for all of five seconds *and* he took care of your mom. How can you not like him?"

"Didn't you notice him staring at your tits the entire time he was talking?"

He was being completely irrational, but now wasn't the time to lay into him. He was already under enough stress as it was. "I'll let that slide because I know you're upset right now. But I just want you to know that under normal circumstances, I'd have punched you in the junk by now."

It felt nice to finally see him laugh. "Duly noted. Come on."

I pulled back slightly when he started for the curtain that concealed his mother from the rest of the area. "Maybe I should just wait out there?" I said, all of a sudden uncomfortable with the idea of seeing his mom. "She might not like other people seeing her like this, you know?"

"Then she shouldn't drink," Luke replied curtly.

I couldn't stand seeing him so angry. He wasn't normally so callous and mean. "Luke, stop. I know you're upset, but she's still your mother."

The angry expression fell from him face, making the stress that lay behind it completely visible. "I need you with me right now," he said quietly. "Is it okay to admit that?"

My heart broke at the lost look shining at me from his eyes. There wasn't much I could deny him at that moment, even if I'd wanted to. "No, it's fine. If you need me, I'll be right there with you." He smiled and lifted my hand to his lips. My heart stopped beating as he pressed a kiss to my knuckles.

I wasn't able to take a breath until he turned away from me to pull the curtain open. "Hey, honey," Mrs. Allen said from the hospital bed. The bandage on her forehead seemed to bring out the dark circles under her eyes. It was a shame she never got help for her drinking, because she really was a beautiful woman. But the years of alcohol abuse had taken a toll on her body. She was too thin and sallow looking, her skin hanging in some places. Her eyes were a little sunken in and her hands shook constantly.

"Hey, Ma. How you feeling?"

"I'm just fine, darling." At that moment, she noticed I was standing behind Luke. "Well, I'll be. Emmy Grace. Aren't you looking beautiful."

I gave her a shy smile. "Hey, Mrs. Allen." I stepped forward next to Luke. "Are you okay?"

She gave me a bright smile, and I couldn't help but smile back. She looked genuinely happy to see me. "I'm fine. Just had a little accident, that's all. How have you been, honey?"

"I've been good, Mrs. Allen."

Just then, the doctor came in with the discharge papers, breaking up the little reunion she and I were having. "Alright, Mrs. Allen, all your scans came back good, so you get to go home. Just take it easy for a few days and try not to get the stitches wet."

"Yes, sir," she replied kindly. "Thank you for everything."

He gave her a warm smile. "My pleasure. Just take better care of yourself. I don't want to have to see you under these circumstances again."

I stifled a laugh when I noticed Mrs. Allen blushing. I wasn't oblivious to the fact that the doctor was a handsome man and clearly neither was she.

He walked over and shook Luke's hand before turning to me and smiling, showing the dimples in his cheeks. "It was lovely meeting you." He pulled a card out of his pocket and handed it to me. "If you ever need anything, please feel free to call me."

Luke stepped beside me possessively as he gave the doctor the stink eye. All I could do was politely take the card and thank him before he left.

The two of us tended to his mother, carefully getting her into Luke's truck and back to her house. Luke got her into bed, and I made her a sandwich so she could take a pain pill. After making sure she was going to be all right, we got back in his truck and headed for the diner.

Luke pulled into the parking lot but didn't bother turning off his truck. "Thanks for sticking with me today," he said. "I can't begin to tell you how much I appreciate that."

I gently touched his forearm. "I already told you, it was no problem. I'm glad I was able to help out." I reached over, opened the door and stepped down. "You going to be okay?"

He gave me a sad smile before mumbling in the affirmative. With no clue what else I could do, I shut the door and stood there, watching as he drove away, and feeling like he was taking a piece of me with him.

CHAPTER TWENTY-ONE

EMERSON

I KNEW I was inviting trouble, but I just couldn't sit back and do nothing. The memory Luke's expression after he dropped me off at the diner the other day was still fresh in my mind.

He hadn't returned to the diner since the morning of his mom's accident and that was two days ago. Jeremy told me that when he ran into him, Luke seemed closed off and didn't hang around any longer than it took to say hello.

I decided that the best thing to do was to pack up a meal and take it to him personally. He'd probably been eating nothing but junk since he wasn't coming to Virgie May's, so a home cooked meal would do him some good, and the diner's meatloaf was the best in three counties. I added some mashed potatoes, green beans, and a slice of Dutch apple pie, then I was off to deliver.

As I pulled into Luke's apartment complex, my stomach started doing somersaults. *I'm just being friendly. I'm just being friendly,* I kept chanting over and over in my head. Logically, I knew I wasn't doing anything wrong, but the more time I spent with him, the more I started to feel that closeness we used to share.

And that terrified me. I felt the walls I'd built to protect my heart crumbling down around him, and I knew that if it kept going like this I was destined for another heartbreak. But I just couldn't stop.

Parking my car, I stepped out and stared up at the dilapidated building that Luke lived in. How anyone could live in a deathtrap like that was beyond me. Pushing those thoughts out of my head, I made my way up the stairs to his front door. When he answered, wearing nothing but a pair of basketball shorts that hung loosely from his waist I nearly swallowed my tongue.

I knew he was ripped, but *what the hell?* I never imagined that amount of muscle was possible on one person. As if that weren't enough, the guy had beads of sweat running between his perfect pecs, all the way down his chiseled abs, past that sexy-as-sin V at his hips and under the waistband of those shorts. The thought of licking sweat off a person's body would have normally made me gag. But I couldn't stop thinking about how badly I wanted to run my tongue from his neck all the way down to his belly button... *and beyond.*

I was in serious freaking trouble.

His deep, masculine chuckle pulled me from my daydream. He totally just busted me lusting after his rock hard body, causing my face to burn six different shades of red. "Enjoying the view, Emmy?" he asked, all cocky and self-assured. And damn him for having every right to be that way.

With a strength I didn't know I had, I managed to drag my gaze away from his torso to his face. "Think you could put a shirt on?" was all I could manage to say.

He crossed his arms over his chest and leaned a shoulder against the doorjamb. *Shit* even his biceps were a sight to behold. "Well now, I don't know if I want to do that. I'm kind of liking this attention."

Shoving him out of the way, and ignoring the way the feel of his skin against mine made me quiver, I pushed into his apartment. "I figured you've been dining on crap for the past couple of days, so I brought you some food. There's enough in here for Trevor if he's hungry."

Luke took the bag from my hand, opened it and sniffed appreciatively. "You're right. I've been living off frozen pizza and ramen, and I'm sick to death of that shit. This smells amazing. What's in here?"

I followed him into the kitchen—or what I could only assume was a kitchen, seeing as it was the size of a closet—and spotted a tattoo on his back as I trailed behind. It was right below his neck, between his shoulder blades. From what I was able to see, it looked like a Celtic knot inlayed in a Maltese cross. It was absolutely beautiful. "Earth to Emmy... you still with me?"

"What? Oh! Um... it's just meatloaf and a few sides. Oh, and I brought you a slice of pie too."

He gave me a sly grin. "What kind of pie?"

I rolled my eyes at his question, like he didn't know I still remembered his favorite kind of pie. "Dutch apple, of course."

"Of course," he said with a wink.

The air between us crackled with a desire I was trying my best to ignore. The temperature in the room went from comfortable to hot and muggy in an instant, causing me to shift uncomfortably from foot to foot. "Well, I should head out and let you and Trev dig in. I'll see you later."

I started for the door when Luke spoke up. "Trevor's not here. He had to head back to Louisiana for the weekend. You want to help me finish this off?" he asked, pointing at the large portions of food in front of him.

"Thanks, but I already ate, so I'm not really hungry."

"That's good because I really didn't want to share any of this... But I'd still like you to stay." I knew I should say no and leave, but my brain and body were saying two totally different things.

I would have liked to think I was a reasonable enough person to listen to my brain but nope... In that moment I was a typical, hormone-driven female. "Okay. Sure, I'll stay for a bit."

We sat and talked for a long time, and it felt nice to be in his company without any animosity hanging over us. We joked and laughed just like we used to. He told me some about his time in the Marines, but I had a feeling he limited the amount he shared because he was afraid of upsetting me. He talked more about his friendship with Trevor and how he ended up as his temporary roommate. My stomach hurt from laughing so hard as Luke told me about some of the shit Trevor had gotten into in the past.

After what seemed like hours, there was finally a lull in the conversation so I broached the subject I'd originally come to talk about. "How's Ilene doing?"

Luke's cheerful demeanor disappeared the second the question cleared my lips. "Fine, I guess," was all he offered, so I dug a little further.

"Have you gone to see her?"

"Yeah." He stood and started to clear dishes from his makeshift table of cardboard boxes. "I've checked on her a few times."

I stood and followed him into the kitchen. The close proximity would've normally bothered me, but something inside me insisted I had to get him talking for his own good. My heart ached and bled for him, knowing how different his life could have been if he had two parents who'd loved and supported him. But he couldn't shut himself off to the pain. I'd tried that myself, and knew that it only led to more in the long run.

"Is she feeling any better?"

He started shoving dishes into the dishwasher so roughly I was sure he'd broken a few. "Of course she's feeling better. She's fucking drunk all day, every day. The woman feels no pain." He slammed the dishwasher closed and placed his hands on the counter in front of him, dropping his head in defeat.

That helpless feeling settled over me again, so I did the only thing I could think of to try and make him feel better. Walking up behind him, I wrapped my arms around his waist, and rested my cheek on his back. His entire body tensed up for just a moment before finally relaxing into my hold. My skin prickled with awareness everywhere it touched his, but I pushed it to the back of my mind, because I knew this closeness was exactly what he needed.

We stood in silence like that for what seemed like an eternity before I finally released him slowly and started to pull away.

I opened my mouth to speak but was immediately cut off when Luke spun around and slammed his mouth down on mine in a hungry kiss. When my lips parted on a gasp, his tongue snaked in, and I was completely lost in the taste and feel of him.

"I don't think we should do this, Luke," I whispered against his lips, some of my sanity managing to break through the haze of lust.

"Please, Emmy. I need this. *I need you*," he begged. It was my undoing.

He sounded so desperate that any rational thoughts I'd had were gone. The only thing I could do was let myself get lost in the kiss.

I pushed up on the balls of my feet and leaned in, trying to get as close as humanly possible, swallowing down the groan Luke released from deep in his throat. I fisted my hands in his hair, pulling him impossibly closer as his desire and need fed my own. Luke followed my direction perfectly, an grabbed my hips to lift me up on the counter. I wrapped my legs around his waist and threw my head back as his lips trailed down my neck to that sensitive spot right below my ear.

The only thing running through my head was that I wanted him more than I'd ever wanted anything. I needed to feel all of him, his skin on my skin, his lips on my lips. I wanted him inside me more than I wanted air. He must have felt the exact same way, because the minute that his lips met my ear, "God I've missed you, Emmy. So fucking bad." The sincerity and longing in his voice pushed my lust into overdrive. He wanted me just as much as I wanted him.

I leaned back just far enough to rip my shirt over my head.

Thank God I wore matching underwear today!

His mouth came down on the upper swell of my breast as his hands snaked under me and lifted me off the counter. He continued his sensual assault as he walked out of the kitchen and into what I could only assume was his bedroom.

I let out a yelp when he tossed me through the air and onto the bed. He was on me instantly, sucking my nipple into a tight peak through the lace of my bra. Arching my back, I tried to bring myself even closer to him as his hand trailed down my stomach to the waistband of my shorts. He had them unbuttoned and was sitting up to remove them when my brain finally decided to join the party. My hands shot down in an attempt to cover the faded scar on my lower stomach but I wasn't fast enough.

"What the hell is that?" he asked, pulling my hands away to study the scar more closely. "Emmy, what happened?"

The look of concern on his face nearly brought tears to my eyes. "It's nothing. I had surgery a few years ago. Please Luke, don't stop." The thought of him pulling away was almost painful. "I need you," I whispered.

He dove back down in a brutal, drugging kiss. "Baby, I need to taste you," he murmured against my mouth.

"*Yes.*"

He kissed his way down my body, removing my bra when

he got to it, then continued further until he reached my panties. He nuzzled his cheek against my inner thigh before slipping a finger past the elastic between my legs and pushing into me. I threw my head back against the pillows and let out an anguished moan. "Christ, you're so wet for me. Tell me you want me, Emmy."

"God, Luke. I want you." What his hand was doing between my legs felt so good, I was having trouble drawing breath. I was on the verge of exploding when he pulled his hand away and jerked my panties off. Before I had a chance to protest, his mouth was on me, teasing my clit as he slipped two fingers back inside me.

"I always knew you'd taste this good. You're so fucking sweet, Emmy." The knot that was coiling in my belly snapped at his words, and I was thrown over the edge into one of the best orgasms of my life. His name was the only word my brain could form as he kept at me, dragging out every ounce of pleasure he possibly could.

My body hadn't even stopped shaking when Luke moved faster than I'd ever seen anyone move. Before I knew it, he was above me resting his weight on his forearms beside my head. "You're so beautiful when you come, baby girl." He entered me with one powerful stroke, stretching me around his thick cock. The combination of pleasure and pain was almost too much to bear.

"*Fuuuuuck.*" He let out a long groan as he pushed in to the hilt. "You're so tight. I don't know how long I'm gonna last. You feel so fucking good."

Instantly, I remembered why it felt so much better than it ever had before. "Condom. Luke, you aren't wearing a condom," I said on an exhale as he continued to move above me.

His eyes met mine, and the emotion I saw in them created a massive lump in my throat. "I'm clean, baby. I swear to God," he said, making it clear he wanted me just like this.

He wanted to feel me with nothing between us, but I'd made that mistake once and I wasn't going to make it again. "I'm not on the pill, Luke."

"Shit," he spat out, finally reaching into the nightstand drawer by his bed. He pulled out of me and quickly rolled the condom down his length. The whole process only took seconds before he was pushing back inside. He stared down into my eyes as he started moving at a pace so fast and hard my body shifted up the bed with each brutal drive of his hips. I felt my climax starting to build back up and lifted my hips to meet him thrust for thrust.

"I've missed you so much, baby," he whispered into my ear and he powered into me, in and out, over and over again until I was right at the edge.

"Oh God. *Luke*. Don't stop."

"Never." He moved faster and faster until, finally, I lost all control. My head flew back, and my eyes screwed shut as the pleasure started to wash over me. "Look at me, baby girl. I want your eyes on mine when you come."

I opened to half mast to meet his, and that was all it took for me to go over. I moaned his name as my body clenched around him.

"So. Fucking. Beautiful," he said, right before he groaned my name with his own release. He buried his face in my neck as we both came down, and the last thing I could recall before slipping into a blissed out sleep was Luke whispering in my ear. "You're mine, Emmy, and I'm not letting you go this time."

CHAPTER TWENTY-TWO

EMERSON

WHEN I BLINKED my eyes open, the room was blanketed in darkness. I was disoriented and unsure of my surroundings until the hard wall against my back shifted. Abruptly, the images of what had happened hours before came crashing down on me like a ton of brinks. I had sex with Luke, the one person I should have stayed far away from. The anxiety came on so strong I almost choked on it.

What the hell was I thinking?

The problem was I *hadn't* been thinking at all. I let my body overrule my brain, and now I was stuck in an impossible situation. I had to get out of there, and fast. Lifting Luke's arm as slowly as I could, I slid out from under it to the edge of the bed. I was feeling around for my clothes when I was suddenly jerked back against his solid chest, his arm like a steel band around my waist.

"Where do you think you're going?" he whispered in my ear before running his tongue along the outer edge and nipping at my lobe.

It felt so damn good my whole body shuddered, but it didn't change anything. "I need to go home," I replied quietly as I stared into the dark. "It's late."

He trailed his lips up and down my neck, and it took all of my willpower to keep myself from melting into him. "I know it's late, so you should just lay back down. Besides, I'm not letting you go anywhere. I'm nowhere near done with you." He rolled me onto my back, climbed between my legs and kissed me like his life depended on it.

I was completely breathless by the time he pulled away and reached over to his nightstand. "Luke, we can't," I said with more conviction than I felt. "We shouldn't have had sex the first time. It was a mistake, and it can't happen again."

His weight disappeared, and the room was suddenly flooded with light. He'd moved so quickly, I hadn't even felt the bed shift before he flipped on the lamp on the nightstand. "A mistake?"

Uh oh.

His anger was palpable, and I couldn't help but cringe at the menacing look on his face. "Did you not hear me last night?" he asked sarcastically.

I pulled the sheet tight against me, using it like a shield in an attempt to cover myself up. "What are you talking about?"

"After I nearly fucked you into a coma I informed you that I wasn't letting you go. Did you somehow miss that?"

His biting tone was quickly feeding my own anger. "Just because you said it, doesn't mean I agree with it. You can't make me do anything I don't want to do, Luke."

The grin that spread across his face was almost frightening. "That's the beauty of it, baby. You want this just as much as I do. You were practically begging for me to be inside you."

"Fuck you," I hissed as I shot off the bed in search of my clothes.

"Oh, I plan to. Over and over." He grabbed me by the arm and pulled me back onto the bed so quick I didn't have time process what was happening. And instant later, his hand was doing unimaginable things between my legs as he kissed me. "Tell me you don't want me," he said as he brought me closer to orgasm. "If you can look me in the eye and say you don't want me, I'll let you go."

I let out a whimper and he pumped his fingers faster. "Luke, please." If I wasn't so close I might have been embarrassed that he could make me beg so easily. But at that point I didn't care about anything except my own release.

"What do you need, baby? Tell me what you need, and I'll give it to you."

"I need…" I couldn't even form a complete sentence. "I need… inside…"

"You need me inside you?"

"Oh God, *yes*."

He quickly donned a condom and turned me on my side. Lifting my leg and placing it over his hip, he entered me from behind so slowly I wanted to cry. I wanted to beg for him to move faster. Just as I opened my mouth to voice my demands, his fingertips skated down my body and began to toy with my clit as he fucked me nice and slow. It was a sensory overload that had me crying out almost instantly.

Luke kept pace, dragging out every last moan and whimper before finally picking up speed and falling over the edge right after.

"SAVANNAH, OPEN UP!" I hollered as I pounded on the door and rang the bell insistently. "Open up! Open up! Open up!"

Her front door flew open, and she stood in front of me in a pair of Hello Kitty boxers, a *Sons of Anarchy* t-shirt, and robe with rubber duckies all over it. "Someone better be dead, Emerson Grace. It's six o'clock in the fucking morning on a Saturday!"

I shoved my way past her and threw myself down on the sofa. "Oh God," I groaned into my hands. "Savvy, I messed up so bad."

"What's going on?" she asked, worry laced through her words as she took a seat beside me. "And why do you have sex hair? Wait..." she inhaled a sharp gasp. "*No!* No, no, no! You didn't."

"Ohgodohgodohgodohgod!"

"How did this happen?" she shrieked.

"I don't know," I shrieked back, then repeated, "I don't know!"

"Why the hell do you keep repeating yourself?"

We were both in freak-out mode. "I don't *fucking know, Savannah!* I can't think right now."

"That's because you just had your brains screwed out!"

With that, I burst into tears.

"Okay. None of that. Come on. Don't cry." Savannah never did well with tears, and her discomfort was evident as she started rubbing my back in an attempt to console me. "I'm sorry I yelled. It's really early. I haven't had coffee and you just told me you had sex. It's too early to process that kind of shit. I'm sorry."

"What the hell was I thinking?" I asked on a sob.

"I don't know, honey."

Wiping at my cheeks, I turned my blurry gaze her way and admitted, "Twice, Savannah. We had sex two times. In one night! I haven't had that much sex in six years!"

She made a face that said *told ya so* clear as day. "I told you that your vow of celibacy was a bad idea. I said that, didn't I? You can't go without for that long, then be around a hot guy and not cave. It's like putting cake in front of a beauty contestant who's been dieting for ten straight years and telling her 'ha ha, you can't eat it'. It's unreasonable."

"This isn't helping *at all*."

Sucking in a huge breath, Savannah scrubbed her hands over her face and asked, "Was it at least good?"

My jaw fell to the floor. "Are you being serious right now?"

"What?" she asked innocently. "It's already done. You can't *un*do it, so you might as well share."

It was sad that I found her reasoning sound. "It was freaking amazing," I admitted painfully. "I want to do it again and again."

She stared at me, unblinking, for several very tense seconds. "Then can you please explain to me why you're at my house at the butt crack of dawn?"

I started twisting my hands in my lap. "I kind of freaked, and snuck out of his bed to run over here."

"I'm sorry," she said, giving her head a vicious shake. "Say what now?"

I threw my hands up in exasperation. "I didn't plan on spending the night, but I kind of fell asleep, then when I woke up and tried to sneak out the first time, *he* woke up and wouldn't let me leave, and we did it again. Then I fell asleep *again* and when I woke up a little while ago, he must have been really worn out because he didn't budge. So I ran over here because I'm losing my mind, and he's going to be *super* pissed when he wakes up and I'm gone, because he already told me that I'm his and he's not letting me go, and he seemed really, really serious." I sucked in a deep breath after spitting all of that out as fast as I possibly could.

Once again, Savannah went completely quiet. But at least this time she blinked. "Well? Aren't you going to say anything?" I finally asked when the silence became unbearable.

"Is it possible to have an orgasm just from listening to you?

Because I think I just totally did."

"*Not helping*!"

"What do you want me to say, Emmy? You tell me you had sex that was so fantastic you passed out not just once, but twice, and that he went all alpha and told you that you were his, and you expect me *not* to have this reaction? Sorry, not possible. That was totally freaking hot! And you know it causes me physical pain to say that, because I hate the jerk."

"What am I going to do, Savvy?"

"I honestly don't know. But you better come up with something fast because if what you say is true, he's going to hunt your ass down once he wakes up.

I was so screwed, and despite what happened the night before, not in the good way. I had so many conflicting emotions that I couldn't tell up from down. On the one hand, I *really* wanted a re-do of what had just transpired between Luke and me, but on the other, I wanted to go home, pack my shit and jump on the first flight to Mexico.

My walls had been completely demolished, and I feared there was no hope of building them back up. I knew it was just a matter of time before he came looking for me, so I needed to come up with a plan...

Fast.

CHAPTER TWENTY-THREE

EMERSON

AROUND NOON, I stupidly decided I didn't need a plan, because there was no way Luke was going to come after me. I was just being ridiculous; this wasn't some *Lifetime* movie where some smoking hot dude I'd just banged "claimed" me, and I had no choice but to bend to his will. This was real life, and real men didn't act that way. I had actually managed to convince myself that if I did run into Luke he would act like nothing happened and we'd go back to the easy friendship we'd started establishing.

I was a freaking idiot.

At a quarter after twelve, Luke came barging into the diner, determination etched into every muscular, chiseled inch of him. "We need to talk. *Now*." He didn't even slow down as he pushed past me and headed in the direction of the office.

Savannah, Stacia, and Lizzy were sitting at a table off in the corner, and when I turned to look at them, they all had startled expressions on their faces. Savannah had already spilled the beans about mine and Luke's little bedroom adventure.

Feeling like I was about to face a firing squad, I turned and started towards the office, taking the trek slowly as I sent a silent prayer heavenward. Not wanting to be left out of the fun, my friends jumped up and followed after me.

I tried to close the door before they reached it, but the three of them pushed their way into the office behind me, their attention bounding between Luke and me like they were watching a tennis match.

"Can we not do this here?" I asked.

He took one menacing step in my direction. I would have backed up if it hadn't been for my soon-to-be-ex friends standing behind me. "If you didn't want to do this here, then you shouldn't have snuck out of my bed in the middle of the fucking night." He didn't raise his voice, but each word that came out of his mouth was no less scary.

"I told you it was late and I needed to go home," I whispered.

"And I specifically remember making it clear that wasn't going to happen."

"Oh shit," Savannah whispered from behind me. She knew his misogynistic attitude would set me off... and she was right.

Slamming my hands on my hips, I breathed fire as I declared, "And I clearly remember saying you can't make me do anything I don't want to do. I didn't want to stay the night in your sorry excuse for a bachelor pad, so I didn't. Do *not* mistake one night of good sex for something else, Lucas."

He got in my face as he hissed his next words. "It was one night of fucking amazing sex... that will be happening again. Trust that. You want to try and hold on to the anger from the past to keep me at a distance, you go right ahead. But I've already set my mind on making things right, and once I set my mind on something, there's no changing it. You're mine, Em. You became mine when you gave yourself to me eight years ago, and you've been mine every day since. I will *not* lose you again. I'm going to get you to forgive me and I *will* earn your trust back. No matter how long it takes."

He grabbed the back of my neck and pulled me to him. There was nothing soft about the kiss he landed on my lips. It was as if he were claiming me right there in front of my friends. When he finally pulled back, I was out of breath and unsteady on my feet. By the time I was able to open my eyes, he'd already walked out the door.

"That was so hot!" Lizzy exclaimed. "You're so right, Savvy. I totally just came."

I hated my friends.

"You're all banned from the diner. For a week!"

"*What*?" Stacia cried.

"Oh, come on!" Savannah pouted.

"*Noooooo!*" Lizzy yelled.

All three of them started whining and complaining instantly.

"And no pie for two weeks. You bitches don't deserve my pie." I turned and headed out of the office toward the front of the diner, the girls hot on my heels.

"You can't do that," Savannah exclaimed. "You know I depend on that pie as a replacement for all the sex I'm *not* having."

"Y'all were no help at all back there, at all!"

"Well, what did you want us to do? He got all possessive and sexy, and we just got sucked into the moment." This came from Stacia.

I cut my eyes in her direction. "You're lucky it's only for a few weeks. I could ban y'all for a month. You're lucky I like you, now get out of my diner."

Savannah stuck her bottom lip out as they headed to the door. "You suck and we aren't friends anymore."

I went back to serving my customers and silently freaking out. I had no clue what I was going to do about the whole Luke thing. He'd made it perfectly clear that he wasn't taking no for an answer, and while part of me wanted to continue to fight the attraction that was burning between us, the other part of me wanted to give in and see where things could go. But I just didn't know if that was a risk I could take. I'd nearly been destroyed the first time around. Was I going to be able to handle it if it went bad again?

No matter how hard I tried, I couldn't come up with an answer to that question.

LUKE

MY DAY HAD STARTED with so much potential. And all of that went down the toilet the minute I rolled over and discovered that I was in my bed, alone, with nothing but the smell of Emmy on my sheets. After searching the apartment and coming up empty, I glanced out the window and saw that her car was gone. "Goddamn it!" Rushing back to my bedroom, I threw on clothes and started for the door when Trevor came walking in.

"Whoa, where's the fire, man?"

"Move out of the way." I tried to shove past him, but his hand clamped down on my arm in a vice grip.

"What's going on? I've never seen you this pissed."

I raked my hands through my hair and stared up at the ceiling. "I swear to Christ. When I find her, I'm gonna cuff her to the goddamned bed *after* I put her over my knee."

"Uh... What the fuck are you talking about?"

I told Trevor about the night before, getting more and more pissed as I thought of her sneaking out of my place before the sun came up.

"Okay, you need to breathe, brother. You can't go after her until you calm the hell down."

"Fuck that. Now move." I pushed him hard, but he stepped back in front of me.

"I'm serious, Luke. If you go after her now, when you're this pissed, you'll end up saying something you can't take back. You need to get your shit straight first."

It was a sad day when Trevor was the voice of reason. I sucked in a few deep breaths, trying to calm my nerves. "Fuck, you're right. I'd likely wring her neck if I saw her right now."

Things hadn't improved any as the day dragged on. I finally felt calm enough to confront Emmy a little after lunch, but that didn't go like I'd hoped. Her demeanor screamed that she was going to fight me at every turn. I spent the rest of my shift in a foul mood, lashing out at everyone who crossed my path.

By the time I got home, all I wanted to do was have a few beers and watch the football game on TV. When Jeremy called me earlier to tell me their band was playing at Colt's I really hadn't wanted to go, but when he informed me that *everyone* was coming I decided that was an opportunity I couldn't pass up.

I could only hope my mood improved before I saw her again.

Because if not, things were liable to go from bad to worse.

CHAPTER TWENTY-FOUR

EMERSON

WALKING into Colt's in my "I'm a groupie and proud of it" t-shirt, I was completely on end. I couldn't shake the sense of dread at the thought of seeing Luke again. Trying to convince myself that I didn't want him was no longer an issue. It wasn't just a physical craving that I felt for him. It was an all-encompassing *need* to be with him. I had stupidly dropped all guards and had fallen in love with the asshole all over again.

"Stop it," Lizzy hissed at me. "You look like you're walking to your execution." I didn't say it out loud, but that was exactly how I was feeling. It was like the countdown had started on how long it would take for him to break my heart all over again.

Not wanting to put a damper on everyone's night, I pasted a smile on my face. "Shut up." I gave her a playful shove. "I still don't like you."

"Whatever. Your pie's not that great anyway."

I leaned back and gasped. "Take that back."

Lizzy looked at me with a smug grin. "No."

"Take it back right this minute, or I'm going to unfriend you on Facebook. And you know that shit's legit."

It was her turn to feign terror. "You wouldn't."

"Just watch me." I pulled the phone out of the back pocket of my skinny jeans, brought up Facebook, and held my finger over the *unfriend* button.

Savannah and Stacia picked that moment to walk up to us. "What's happening right now?" Stacia asked. "This looks intense."

Neither Lizzy nor I broke eye contact. "This bitch is threatening to unfriend me."

"What? *Why?*" In Stacia's world, being unfriended was one of the worst things that could possibly happen.

"She said my pie wasn't that great."

Both Savannah and Stacia took a step back. "Them's fightin' words, Lizzy," Savannah told her.

I started to count down. "Five... four... three..."

"All right, all right! I take it back. You've got the best pie in all the land."

Stacia let out a relieved sigh at Lizzy's surrender.

"Damn straight I do," I said with a triumphant smile.

"Now that that's over with, can we please get up to the stage so I can see my man play?"

I turned to Stacia and laughed. "Did you bring your panties this time?"

"Damn it!" she said as she stomped her foot. "I knew I forgot something."

The four of us laughed as we made our way to our coveted spot at the front of the stage. As the night wore on and Luke didn't show, I slowly started to relax. The four of us drank, danced, and sang along to every song the guys played. I was in the middle of some serious ass shaking as they played The Ataris version of "The Boys of Summer," when I felt a pair of hands snake around my hips. "Jesus Christ, baby, do you have any clue how fucking good you look when you dance?"

My brain instantly malfunctioned as Luke whispered in my

ear. It felt so damn good to have him wrapped around me.

I started to pull away, but he grabbed my shoulders and spun me around so I was facing him. "What do you think you're doing?" I asked as he slid his hands over my ass.

"What's it look like I'm doing?" he said in my ear as he traced his tongue along the sensitive cord of my neck. "I'm dancing with my girl."

"I'm not your girl," I mumbled weakly. I might have said the words, but nothing about my body language backed them up. I latched on to the front of his blue button-down as he slid his thigh between my legs. *God*, everything about this man felt good.

"In a few minutes, I bet I can get you singing a different tune."

In a few minutes, I was going to be a big puddle of goo on the dance floor. "Luke," I tried to protest.

He brushed his lips gently against mine to silence me. "Just dance with me, baby girl. I just need to feel you in my arms."

How could I say no to that? We spent several songs wrapped up in each other. Even though my brain's initial reaction was to fight it, I couldn't get past the feeling that it seemed right just to be held by him.

"Do you know how much I missed you?" he asked me as we swayed to one of the slower songs.

I buried my face in his neck to hide the tears. "Then why'd you leave?" My voice broke at the end of the sentence, and Luke ran his fingers through my hair in a calming gesture.

"Because I was stupid," he stated matter-of-factly. "I loved you so damn much, but I thought I was no good for you. I swear to Christ, Emmy, I really thought I was doing what was best for you."

I pulled out of his neck and stared up at him in shock. "You loved me?"

He smiled down at me as he trailed his fingers down my cheek. "I still do, baby girl. You're the only reason I came back."

I shook my head in disbelief as more tears fell. Luke wiped them away and pressed his lips to mine, and this time I didn't bother protesting. I wanted the kiss as much as he did, and I was done denying it.

We stayed that way until the sound of a throat clearing behind us broke into the personal moment. I pulled back and looked over my shoulder to see all my girlfriends and Trevor staring. Savannah looked a little concerned but the rest of them all had shit-eating grins on their faces, Trevor included. God, that guy could be such a chick sometimes.

"Sorry to interrupt," Trevor said with a chuckle, proving he wasn't sorry at all. "But we're heading to the bar. Y'all feel like joining, or you going stand here and suck face a little while longer?"

Luke took my hand and started leading me to the bar with the others. "You want a place to live?" he asked threatening as we walked past Trevor.

"Just feeling the love, man. That's all. It's really inspiring."

"Feel it silently." I couldn't help but laugh at the interaction between Luke and Trev. At times, they seemed like an old married couple. I could see why the two of them had formed such a tight bond. I was glad they had each other to lean on when they were over seas.

We got to the bar, and I glanced over to Savannah, noticing that she'd gotten unnaturally quiet. I started to pull away from Luke but his hand tightened on mine. When I turned my attention to his face I saw the question in his eyes. "I'm just going to talk to Savannah." He gave me a smile and let go, but not before delivering yet another bone-melting kiss.

When he finally released me and my legs started cooperating again, I made my way over to my best friend. "Hey, sweetie. What's on your mind?"

She plastered on a fake smile. "Once I get a beer, not a damn thing."

My lips dipped into a worried frown. "You really want me to call you on that lie?"

"No," she answered on a sigh. "Look, I'm really trying to be supportive of this whole Luke and you kissing thing. I just can't help but be concerned, you know?"

Giving her a big hug, I whispered in her ear, "I know babe, believe me. But I tried ignoring what's happening between me and Luke, and it just didn't work."

She squeezed me back tightly. "I know, Emmy. And I'm happy if you're happy."

I gave that statement some thought. "You know what?" I asked, surprised by my sudden epiphany. "I really am."

We talked for a few more minutes before her smile dropped and her happy demeanor turned vicious. "Can we have just one night without that walking STD ruining everything?"

Spinning on my platform wedges, I looked to see what she was talking about, and the world beneath my feet disappeared at the sight of Allison draped over the front of Luke. In his defense, it appeared that he was trying his hardest to detach her talons, but the bitch wouldn't budge.

"Seriously? You've got to be kidding me," I mumbled before calling out. "Hey Luke, you've got a little bit of trash stuck to the front of your shirt."

Luke's lips quirk up and Trevor choked on his beer before he busted out laughing. Allison wrinkled her nose at me and turned away.

"You might want to get your hands off her man before she breaks your fingers," Lizzy warned as I walked up next to Luke and slipped my arm through his.

"Her man? You've *got* to be joking. Luke, please tell me you have better taste than that."

Luke finally managed to remove her hands from his shirt and stepped into me. "You need to move along."

Allison turned her evil sneer in my direction as she said, "When you're done slumming, you have my number."

She started to turn away but I just couldn't help myself. "You know Allison, if you quit doing your makeup like a two-dollar crack whore, maybe guys would quit banging you doggy style and actually look you in the eye."

When her hate filled eyes cut to me, the hair on the back of my neck stood on end. "Oh, that's hilarious coming from you."

My back went straight. "What's that supposed to mean?"

"At least I'm not so pathetic I'd try and trap a guy by getting knocked up."

All of the blood drained from my face. I couldn't move or speak as Luke looked at me with wide, bewildered eyes. "What the fuck is she talking about, Emmy?"

"You *bitch*!" Savannah screamed. "You did *not* just say that!" She lunged at Allison before anyone could react, punching her right in the face. The two of them hit the ground in a pile of hair and flailing limbs. Allison shrieked as Savannah connected with her jaw for a second time.

It was like someone had hit a button on a remote, and everything was suddenly moving in slow motion. It felt like an eternity had passed before my legs finally started working again, but once they did I ran for the door like the hounds of hell were nipping at my heels. I knew Luke wasn't far behind but I had to get out. I couldn't breath. The walls were closing in on my, sucking out all the air.

"*Emmy!*" Luke shouted as he ran after me. He caught up easily enough, and latched onto my elbow spinning me around with a bone jarring jerk. "What the *fuck* is she talking about?" he bellowed, making me wince.

I couldn't form a sentence as Luke glared down at me, seething with anger. I tried pulling my arm away but his grip only tightened.

"Let her go, Luke. Right now." After Allison's latest stunt, I'd been so focused on my escape that I hadn't noticed all of my friends following us out of the bar.

Brett came up next to me and tried to get Luke's attention. "I'm serious, man. Let her go."

"Come on buddy, lets all just take a breath." Trevor was standing behind him trying to talk him down gently, but Luke wasn't having any of it.

"Who got you pregnant, Emmy?" His hushed tone scared me more than when he was yelling. "Answer me!"

"I said let her go!" Brett shouted.

"This is none of your fucking business, Brett. This is between me and Emmy."

"Not when you're yelling at her like this, man. Just calm down."

Luke looked at Brett then back at me. "Fuck calm! Who got you pregnant, Emmy?"

The lump in my throat threatened to choke me, but I somehow managed to croak out an answer. "You did," I whispered.

Luke took a step back, dropping my arm like it burned him. After a minute of heavy silence, he finally asked, "Where's my kid, Emerson?"

A sob ripped it's way from my chest. Savannah must have finished her fight with Allison at some point, because at that moment, she stepped up next to me and wrapped her arms around my shoulders. "Luke, you need to relax, okay? This is not the time for this conversation."

He let out a humorless laugh. "Not the time? *Not the time?* Are you fucking kidding me? I just found out she had my kid, and I never fucking knew about it! Where the fuck is my kid, Emmy? Did you get rid of it?"

All the fear I felt just moments ago left my body. Something inside me withered and died, and was replaced with an all too familiar icy numbness. The fact that he could accuse me of something so horrible told me exactly the kind of guy he really was. He hadn't changed at all; he was still as much of an asshole now as he was then.

"Stand down, Luke, before I knock you on your fucking ass." Brett might not have been as tall as Luke, but what he lacked in height, he made up for in bulk. A fight between those two would be evenly matched and equally deadly.

"Did you get rid of my kid, Emerson? Just pawn it off on someone else? I swear to Christ, if you gave my child up without my permission, I'm taking your ass to court."

That was it. Brett's patience snapped with that one statement. The only sounds I could make out over the blood rushing through my ears were those of flesh hitting flesh as Luke and Brett worked their hardest to rip each other to pieces. All I could do was stand, frozen in shock as two of the people I'd known my whole life beat the hell out of each other. I vaguely recalled the screams of my friends begging them to stop as I stared at the destruction in front of me.

Trevor and Jeremy finally pushed their way in, and pulled the two of them apart. Brett was sporting a busted lip and Luke had a nasty looking gash through his left eyebrow. Both of them had bruises that were swelling up all over their faces.

"Calm down!" Gavin yelled, trying to get the two men to stop lunging at one another.

"I'm going to kill you, you motherfucker!" Brett shouted. "Don't you *ever* talk to her like that. *Do you hear me?*"

Luke struggled against Trevor's hold with everything he had. "What the hell do you expect me to think, Brett? I get back after eight fucking years, and find out she had my kid and *I never knew!*"

All at once, Brett stopped fighting against Jeremy, and I could see his grip loosening. "Whose fault is that, asshole? You never picked up your phone or answered a single goddamn email from any of us. You want to know where your kid is? Visit Cloverleaf Cemetery."

"Brett," Savannah said with a ragged whisper. "*No.*"

Everyone around me stopped moving, including Luke. "What?" he asked as all the fight drained out of him.

"You threw out accusations without even thinking. You know Emmy, probably better than any of us. Did you, even once, think about how she might have suffered through after you abandoned her? You don't deserve her forgiveness, but she gave it to you anyway, and you repay her like this? That baby was the only thing that got her through you leaving, and when she lost it we were all terrified out of our fucking minds that we'd lose her too."

Brett stopped long enough to shake his head and curl his lip in disgust before issuing his parting shot. "You never should have come back. You're fucking toxic."

With that, Brett turned and walked away.

CHAPTER TWENTY-FIVE

EMERSON

AFTER BRETT WALKED AWAY, everyone stood there staring between Luke and me. Savannah and Lizzy had tears in their eyes. Jeremy just hung his head. Gavin and Stacia held on to each other, and Trevor shuffled from foot to foot. Luke was completely motionless for what felt like years before he finally addressed me.

"Emmy, I—"

I moved to stand directly in front of him. "I didn't 'get rid' of your kid, Luke. *You* never had a kid. *I* did. You lost all rights to my child when you refused to answer my calls or emails so I could tell you I was pregnant. I had a baby that I loved more than anything in this world, and I lost her."

"Her?" he asked, tears welling up in his eyes. "It was a girl?"

"Yes," I answered, my voice cold and emotionless.

He raked his hands through his hair and hung his head. "Jesus Christ. Emmy, baby..."

He reached for me, but I took a huge step back. "Don't touch me," I hissed. "From this moment on, you don't ever touch me. You don't look at me. You don't fucking talk to me. I want nothing to do with you, Luke. You're nothing but poison, so as far as I'm concerned you no longer exist."

"You don't mean that. Please, Emmy—"

"I mean it." I felt nothing but numbness filling that space where my heart used to be, and it reflected in my tone. I was so through with Luke. "I never thought I could possibly hate a person as much as I hate you. Accusing me of getting rid of my child just proved to me what a piece of shit you really are. You and Allison deserve each other. You're both bottom feeders."

I turned and walked away, not giving him a chance to say anything else.

"Emmy, sweetie, wait up," Savannah called as she ran after me. "Are you okay?"

I opened my car door and climbed in as I answered. "I'm so far from okay it's not even funny. I'm done with this shit, Savvy. I'm going home."

Her eyes were frantic and pleading as she said, "Let me come with you. Please, honey. You don't need to be alone right now."

I placed my hand on her arm to try and calm her down. "I'm okay, Savannah. I won't do anything stupid, I promise. I just really want to be by myself."

"Are you sure?"

I gave her a sad smile and responded, "Yeah, I'm sure. I'll call you tomorrow, okay?"

I could tell she didn't want to let me go. She was afraid I'd sink back down into the dark place I'd lived in after I lost my daughter. I was in a bad way, but I'd never let myself go there again.

It had taken a long time, but I knew now that I was so much stronger. Life knocked me down, but I always got back up.

And this time wouldn't be any different.

LUKE

BY THE TIME I got my shit together and ran after Emmy, I was too late. Her car was just pulling away and Savannah was staring after it as tears streamed down her face. I came to a stop when she spun around to face me.

"You son of a bitch! I knew you'd do this to her!" She slapped me so hard my head shot to the side, stars bursting behind my eyelids. I finally understand Savannah's hatred, and I deserved every bit of it.

"I'm sorry," I whispered pathetically. I didn't know what else to say.

"You're sorry? Oh, that just makes everything better, doesn't it? How in the hell could you think she'd give up her own baby?"

"I wasn't thinking," I replied. "*Fuck*! I know she wouldn't do something like that, but I was just so... God, I fucked up. How do I fix this, Savannah? I know you hate me, but you have to help me fix this." I'd never felt more desperate in my life.

"I'm not helping you with shit. I wanted so bad to think you really were capable of changing, but tonight you just proved me right. You are the worst human being on the face of the earth, Luke. Stay the fuck away from Emmy."

She started to walk away, but I grabbed onto her arm. "I'm *begging* you, Savannah. Please, at least tell me what happened."

She remained silent for several seconds, indecision warring in her eye, but when she didn't walk away, I knew she'd give me what I'd asked for. I just didn't know that hearing it would wreck me beyond repair.

"The doctor called it placental abruption. She was nine-months pregnant when she started bleeding heavily." Savannah's face went pale as she spoke, and her voice started to shake.

"I tried to get her to the hospital as fast as I could, but we didn't make it in time. The baby died, and we almost lost Emmy because of all the blood she lost."

My heart shattered into a million pieces as I let out an agonized, "Holy shit."

"She didn't even get a chance to hold her daughter before she had to put her in the ground. Now you see why you need to get the hell out of her life? Everything about you is a reminder of what she lost." She pulled her arm out of my grasp and started walking again. I didn't stop her this time. "You aren't good for her, Luke," she called over her shoulder as she moved away, leaving me standing alone with my thoughts. That wasn't a good place for me to be at the moment.

When I got back to my truck I was surprised to see Trevor still standing there. "You okay, man?" he asked as I got closer.

"No," I stated. "I'm so fucking far from okay, it's unreal." He nodded his head but remained silent. "Lizzy told you what happened, didn't she? With the pregnancy?"

Trevor let out a long sigh before answering. "Yeah. When you ran after her, Lizzy filled me in. It was bad, brother. I mean *really* bad."

"Savannah told me about the bleeding and Emmy almost dying."

"There's more to it than that. I didn't get the long and drawn out of it, but from what Lizzy said, I gather that Emmy was in a real bad head space for a while after the baby died."

I rubbed my hands over my face and looked up at the black sky. "Could this night get any fucking worse?"

"I don't see how." Trevor walked up and placed a supportive hand on my shoulder. "Nothing more you can do tonight, Luke. Let's head home. You can get some sleep and maybe come up with a plan in the morning."

I looked at Trevor and let out a dry laugh. "I don't see me

coming back from this one, Trev."

He shook his head and gave me a look of pity. "I hope you're wrong, but I just don't know."

CHAPTER TWENTY-SIX

EMERSON

PAST

"MAYBE YOU SHOULDN'T BE STANDING up there. You said yourself that you were feeling a little pain."

Savannah was holding the bottom of the ladder for me as I reached up to paint the last white butterfly on Ella's lavender nursery wall. I wanted to make her room as beautiful and girly as possible, so I went with soft purple walls with white and pink butterflies strategically placed all around. The people who wrote the books on pregnancy weren't joking when they said the mother started nesting near the end of her pregnancy. I was nine months along, due in just a matter of weeks, and when I woke up that morning the need to finish my daughter's room just wouldn't be denied.

I wished Grams could have been here, but she was at the diner, so I called Savannah over to help me finish up the last of it.

I was so anxious to meet my sweet baby girl. I couldn't wait to get Ella home and see her swaddled in her pretty pink baby blanket. I could already picture myself sitting in the glider as I rocked her peacefully in my arms.

"It's just Braxton Hicks, Savvy. The doctor said it was totally normal at this stage in the pregnancy. Now shut up and hand me that stencil."

She huffed out a frustrated breath but finally relented and did as I ordered. I reached down to get the butterfly stencil when a sharp pain cut through my abdomen. It hurt so bad it took my breath away and nearly took me off my feet and I had to cling to the top rung of the ladder so I wouldn't fall. I thought I could wait out the pain, but after counting down a minute, it still hadn't subsided.

"What's happening? Emmy, what's wrong?" Savannah asked in a rush, clearly freaking out.

It was almost unbearable, but I did my best to climb down the ladder and curled up on the nursery floor. I was trying to do the deep breathing I'd read about in one of my books, but the pain wasn't getting any better "I don't know what's wrong, but this isn't right. God, it hurts." To make matters worse, when I looked up at Savannah she'd gone ghostly white. Something was very wrong. These weren't just normal labor pains.

"Oh God, Emmy, you're bleeding!"

"*What?*" When I tried to sit up to see what she was talking about the room started to spin around me. "Savvy," I mumbled through the pain. "I need you to drive me to the hospital. We have to go right now."

"Emmy, I need to call an ambulance. There's too much blood." Tears spilled from Savannah's eyes as she spoke.

"We can't wait for an ambulance," I sobbed, continuing to beg, "That'll take too long. Please, just help me up. We have to go."

Savannah didn't hesitate. She pulled me from the floor just as another stabbing pain ripped through my stomach. It was a miracle that I made it to Savannah's car without passing out, but the desperation to keep my baby safe pushed me to keep going. As I sat in the passenger seat I tried my hardest to keep my eyes open, but with each passing second it became harder and harder. Everything seemed to be slowing down, and my vision began to blur. The last thing I remembered before passing out was reaching down to stroke my stomach as tears streamed down my face.

"It's okay, baby," I spoke to my belly. "Mommy's going to get you through this. Just hang on, Ella. I love you." After that, everything went black.

I WOKE up groggy and out of sorts. Nothing around me felt familiar. I blinked several times trying to get my vision in focus. "She's awake." I heard from somewhere next to me. It sounded like Savannah but I couldn't be sure. It felt like my brain was taking forever to kick-start. "Emmy, sweetie, can you hear me?"

Savannah's face came into my line of sight, blurry and out of focus. "What happened?" I asked in a voice so scratchy I barely recognized it. It hurt to speak.

"Oh, honey." Savannah broke down in gut wrenching sobs. I saw movement from behind her and watched Jeremy pull her into a hug. A quick glance around showed that Grams, along with all of my friends, were standing around me.

The memories of where I was and why came rushing back. I quickly reached down to caress my stomach, terror running through me when it felt smaller than it had been before. "Where's Ella?" I asked on a choked hiccup. "Where's my baby?"

Grams came and sat on the side of my bed, taking my hand in hers. "Baby," she whispered as her face crumbled. "There was a complication that the doctors weren't expecting." She cleared her throat before continuing. "Emmy, you started bleeding because your placenta detached. Ella didn't make it, sweetie. I'm so sorry."

Never in my life had I seen my grandmother so heartbroken. Even when my parents died, she'd been my rock. Seeing her breakdown in tears was just too much.

"But... I don't understand. She has to be okay. I just finished her nursery. She hasn't even had a chance to sleep in it yet."

Lizzy let out a loud cry and ran from the hospital room. "Where is she?" I managed to ask past the lump in my throat. "How long have I been out?"

Brett came up to me then, and tucked a strand of hair behind my ear. "Emmy, you were in ICU for a day. They had to do emergency surgery to stop the bleeding. You've been in and out for three days."

I lost it then. Knowing my daughter had died three days ago, and I didn't get to hold her was more painful than anything else. Not being able to hold her or kiss her little cheeks ripped my insides apart. My friends and Grams just held on to me as I wailed and screamed so hard my chest hurt. I cried until there weren't any tears left. The nurse came in to push more pain meds, and after what felt like hours of agonizing torment, I was finally forced to sleep. But when I woke later that evening, I remembered... *everything.* The torture started all over again. It was a vicious circle that lasted weeks.

After the tears disappeared, the numbness invaded.

I sat through my daughter's funeral in complete silence, unable to acknowledge anyone. That feeling lasted longer than the soul ripping sadness. I went through my days like a zombie, not caring about anything or anyone. I felt like an empty shell of my former self. The door to Ella's nursery was shut and remained that way for over a year. It was never to be touched.

Eventually, the emptiness wore off and depression took over. I found that I could easily drown it out if I drank enough. So, that was exactly how I spent the next year of my life. There wasn't a day that passed where I didn't remember the loss of my daughter. I drank to numb the pain. I drank to forget. I drank because I hated myself. I drank because I hated everyone. I drank because, plain and simple, I hated everything about my life.

PRESENT

REMEMBERING that part of my life made me cringe. I was embarrassed of who I'd been, and I never wanted to be that person again. I went out to the bars in the city every night and met people who didn't know me, who didn't know about my past or that I was drinking and partying to fill a void. I hung around some really bad people that did some pretty bad stuff, but I didn't care. They supplied the drugs and alcohol, so as far as I was concerned, they were just fine.

I knew that what I was doing wasn't really who I was, but being drunk or high was better than being sad. My friends tried so hard to be supportive, but every time I looked at them, I could see the pity in their eyes, and I hated it. I couldn't stand to be around anyone who knew.

I was ashamed of the downward spiral I was on, but I didn't know how to pull myself out of it. God only knew how long it would have lasted if I hadn't hit rock bottom as soon as I did. I woke up one morning in a room I didn't recognize, lying in a bed with two men that I didn't know. I couldn't remember what happened the night before, but from the lack of clothing on all three of us, it was easy to figure out what I had done.

I'd jumped out of the bed, ran to the bathroom and emptied my stomach of all its contents. When I was finally able to move from the floor, I dressed as quickly as possible and ran out of the room. When I found out I was in some shitty hotel, in an even shittier part of town, I hesitated for only a moment before calling Savannah to come get me. It was the first time in a year I'd asked for her help, and she was there the moment I needed her.

It took a lot of work, but I managed to get my shit together and started pulling myself up with the help of the people who loved me. There was no doubt in my mind that they were terrified I'd revert back to that girl after my blow up with Luke. But I knew I was tougher than that.

The ringing of my phone pulled me out of my thoughts and back to reality. I grabbed my cell from the nightstand and looked at the display before answering the call. "Good morning, Savannah," I said in lieu of *hello*. "I'm still fine."

"I don't know what you're talking about," she replied snottily. "I'm not calling to check on you. There's a *Supernatural* marathon on today, and I just thought you'd want to know, that's all."

I let out a deep belly laugh. "Much appreciated, love. Tell you what. Why don't you see if all those people standing beside you want to come over, and we can watch it together?"

"People? What people? I'm here all by my lonesome." I could hear the laughter in her voice and it made me smile even more.

"Am I on speaker?"

She hesitated, then finally answered, "Maybe."

"Lizzy, Brett, Stacia, Gavin, and Jeremy. Would you like to join me and Savannah for a *Supernatural* marathon today?"

Different versions of yes came from all of my friends in the background. "You guys suck," Savannah told them. "So much for covert."

I heard a throat clear in the background. "Uh...Emmy? Trevor here," he said quietly.

I couldn't help but smile. "Hey, Trev."

"You doing okay, gorgeous?" I loved how Trevor managed to pull off flirting in any scenario.

"I'm good, Trev. You?"

"Well. Uh... I was wondering—seeing as I love *Supernatural* and all—"

"You coming alone?" I interrupted.

"That can be arranged," he responded. He still considered Luke his best friend, but over the past several weeks it had become clear that wherever Lizzy went, Trevor followed.

"Then do you want to come over to watch it?" I asked.

"Well, I guess I could squeeze you in..."

I let out another laugh and addressed the whole group. "You guys are ridiculous. I'll see you in thirty. Bring food!" I hung up and climbed out of my bed feeling a little bit lighter. Luke wasn't going to destroy me this time. I spent massive amounts of time worrying about how I would handle it when he broke my heart again. It felt like a weight being lifted off my chest to know I'd be just fine.

CHAPTER TWENTY-SEVEN

LUKE

LYING under my mom's kitchen sink with a hangover was *not* how I imagined I'd be spending my one day off. I fully intended to be in my bed, blinds closed and covers over my head, nursing the headache that bitch, Johnny Walker, had given me. But what could I do? Ma called me to ask if I could fix a leaky faucet, and she'd sounded more with it than I'd heard in years. So there I was.

"You okay, honey? You don't look so good."

Luckily, she couldn't see me rolling my eyes from under the sink. "Just fine, Ma."

"Really?" she asked. The sarcastic tone in her voice was unexpected. "Because if there's one thing I know, it's a hangover. And you, son, are working one killer hangover."

I let out a loud sigh and gave the wrench one last crank, sealing the pipe closed. Wriggling my way from beneath the sink, I sat with my elbows on my bent knees. "No offense, but it's not something I really want to talk about right now."

"Hmm," was the only response I got. I'd just finished tossing the last of my tools in my toolbox when she finally spoke again. And what she said stopped me in my tracks. "So I'm guessing you found out about Emmy's baby?"

What the hell? "You knew about that?" I shot up off the kitchen floor and stalked over to the table where she was sitting.

"Well, it *is* a small town, Lucas."

"Why the hell didn't you tell me?" I shouted. "You're my mom, you're supposed to tell me shit like that!"

Her voice was as sharp as a tack when she commanded, "Sit down. Now." I'd never heard that much authority in her voice before. I sat my ass in a chair at her kitchen table, just like she told me to do. When I finally met her eyes, I saw something that made the air whoosh out of my lungs. Her green eyes were actually sparkling, not glazed over like they had been every day since I was old enough to notice. *Holy shit. She's sober.*

"I'm going to tell you something, and I don't want any interruptions." Why hadn't I noticed there was no slurring in her speech until now? I was dumbstruck by what I was seeing, so all I was able to manage was a nod. "I didn't do right by you, Lucas. I know that. Hell, I've known that for a long time."

I felt like I was in the fucking Twilight Zone.

She continued on. "I've been a shitty mother..." She held up her hand when she noticed me open my mouth to speak. "... and I don't deserve it, but I'm going to ask for your forgiveness anyway. I should have stopped your father all those times he raised his hand to you. It wasn't right, hitting a defenseless child like that. I should have been strong enough to kick his worthless ass out of my house long before he left.

"The things you saw and dealt with..." She sucked in a breath, trying to hold back the tears shining in her eyes. "God. You never should have lived like that. Then me being a drunk..." There it was. Mom had finally admitted it, after all these years. She couldn't hold the tears back any longer. As she talked, her voice broke. "You're not him, baby." That statement hit me like a punch to the gut. "You are not your father, Luke. Do you understand me? You are so much stronger than he ever was. The kindness in your heart makes you the man you are. You don't have one single ounce of him in you."

It was too much. Everything she was saying was just too much. I was barely functioning thanks to my hangover. I couldn't handle this. She must have seen it written on my face, because she continued. "I'm getting help, baby."

My head shot up, and my breathing became erratic. I had hoped for this moment for so long.

"I found a place in Houston. I'm going to rehab. Then I figured I'd sell the house and see about getting myself a cute little apartment. I'm going to get myself cleaned up, and I'm going to be the mother you deserve. I know you're grown now, and you probably don't need me anymore, but I'm still going to do this. For the both of us."

I was out of the chair faster than I'd ever moved. Getting on my knees in front of her, I grabbed my mom and wrapped her in a hug so tight I was afraid I might crush her. When I went to loosen my arms hers clenched tighter, refusing to let go.

"I'll always need you, Ma. Never doubt that. I'm so goddamned proud of you." I felt myself having to choke back a riot of emotions as I held onto her with all my strength.

After what seemed like forever, she pulled back and went about wiping her face. Seemingly composed, she pointed back to the chair I'd vacated, indicating I needed to sit back down, because she wasn't finished. "All right," she started then cleared her throat. "Having said everything I just said, you and I are about to have a little come-to-Jesus, son."

Shit. This can't be good.

"Yes, I knew about the pregnancy. Now, I might be a drunk, but that doesn't mean I'm an idiot. I heard the rumors and I saw that poor girl, walking around completely heartbroken. I was so damn mad at you when I found out what you did. I could have spit nails. And the more time that went by, the madder I got." Mom leaned in close, her facing going sad all of a sudden. "She was sick, Lucas. Real sick. It was obvious that pregnancy wasn't easy on her. But God bless that child, she tried." Hearing my mom talk about how bad things had been made me want to die a thousand times.

"She and I were never close, you know that. She was such a good friend to you. I knew she hated me for everything I put you through, but that doesn't mean I ever hated her. I've always held Emmy in a special place in my heart because of what she was for you. I always thought you two would end up married one day." I hung my head in shame at my mother's words. "It might sound bad, but I wasn't surprised when I found out she was pregnant with your baby. But it did shock me when I found out you just up and left her. Especially the way you did it."

She reached over and placed her hand on top of mine. "I was mad, baby... but I understand why you did it." I looked at her skeptically. "You were afraid you were him. And you were scared that if you stayed, you'd break Emmy, like he broke me."

My head jerked back, startled at how spot-on my mother was. Who was this amazing woman in front of me? "But you see, you and Emmy could never be like me and your dad. Not only because you aren't your father, but because Emmy isn't me. She's got a will of steel. That girl is so strong, Luke, you wouldn't believe it. She doesn't have it in her to break the way I did. She might have had a rough go of it for a while, but that child pulled herself back up and powered through."

"You're powering through, Ma. You're strong too."

She looked at me with a sad smile. "Not strong like that, baby. The girl has gone through so much more sadness than any person deserves to in their whole life, and look at her. She still walks through this town with her head held high. She's inspirational."

Sucking in a deep breath, I asked the question I was dreading the answer to. "Was it bad... the... when she lost..." I didn't have the strength to continue.

Mom twined her fingers with mine. "Yeah, baby. It was bad... for a while."

I felt the tears burning the back of my throat. "God, Ma. I've fucked up so bad. I don't think I'll ever be able to fix it. She hates me."

Reaching up and cupping my face in her hands, my mom said something that would stick with me until the day I died. "She doesn't hate you, baby. She loves you. And she's mad as all hell about that. That just proves that you have something left to fight for. You're the strongest man I know, Lucas. You fight for her. That girl became your other half the day we moved into this house. She'll be your other half 'til the day you die, and you'll be hers. You get her back, and y'all can finally start living your lives whole."

I left my mother's house a little while later feeling better than I had in longer than I could remember. Getting Emmy to forgive me was going to be the hardest thing I'd ever done, but my mom was right. I wasn't complete without her. My life wouldn't mean anything if she wasn't in it. I had a plan but no one to help since all of my "friends" made it clear where I stood as far as Emmy was concerned. Jeremy and Gavin might not hate me as much as the others did, but it was still pretty evident that they didn't think I was good enough for Emmy, not that I could blame them.

I *wasn't* good enough for her.

No man ever would be, but she was mine, and I was hers. And I was going to spend the rest of my life making her happy. But something told me that outrunning sniper fire would be easier than what I had to do next. Going to Savannah for help was like walking into a lion's den wearing a meat suit, but I had to do what I had to do.

Because Emmy was worth it.

CHAPTER TWENTY-EIGHT

EMERSON

MY PHONE HAD BEEN RINGING off the hook for the past week. Luke was relentless with his calls and texts. I almost considered changing my number, but knowing he was suffering now just as much as I had all those years ago when I couldn't get a hold of him made the constant ringing worth it. I deleted each text and voicemail without opening them.

I threw myself into the diner and worked so many hours that by the time I got home, I was so exhausted all I could do was fall into the bed and sleep until it was time to wake up and do it all over again. It wasn't the healthiest way of handling things, but it worked better than booze or drugs, that was for damn sure.

When the bell over the door rang, I looked up to greet the next customer. "Mrs. Allen?" I asked as Luke's mom came walzing through the door. "How are you?" I walked up to the older woman and immediately realized something was different. Her smile was bright, and I'd never seen her so clear-eyed. She looked twenty years younger, and *happy*.

"I'm good, sweetie, how are you?"

I smiled in return, feeling her happiness rubbing off on me.

"I'm doing okay. You look wonderful today. Did you do something different with your hair?"

She reached up and ran her hand over her black tresses, the streaks of gray making it look as if it was highlighted with a very attractive silver. "Oh, no, nothing different."

I tilted my head to the side and studied her more closely. "What did you do different?"

She let out cheerful laugh and grabbed a hold of my hand. "Why don't we have a seat and talk for a minute?"

I followed her over to one of the tables in front of the window and sat across from her. Although she and I had never been close, I had grown up around her, so it was easy to see the change in her.

"How you doing, sugar?" she asked again.

I let out a small laugh. "I'm good, Mrs. Allen." I wasn't exactly sure why she was repeating the question, but I had a sneaking suspicion that I was in for a really uncomfortable conversation.

"Please, call me Ilene." She sat there looking at me for a few moments before speaking again. I got the distinct feeling that she was studying me to see if my response was honest. That got my hackles up. "You sure about that, Emmy?" she asked, causing my spine to straighten in defense.

"What do you mean?" I tried to sound casual, but I knew I'd failed at pulling it off.

"I'm going to be honest with you right now. I know about everything that happened between you and Luke."

I didn't want to have this conversation at all, let alone with Luke's mother. "Mrs. Allen" I started but she quickly interrupted.

"Please Emmy, call me Ilene, and before you go on the defensive, I just want you to know I'm not here to lecture. God knows I've got no business judging anyone on the choices they make." She took a deep breath before continuing. "I just wanted to let you know that I know what you went through, and it probably doesn't matter for much, but I just wanted you to tell you that I'm so damn proud of you."

I was taken aback by her declaration. I wasn't sure what brought it on, but hearing her say that was very moving. The tears in her eyes caused me to choke up as well.

"Thank you, Ilene," I whispered. "That means a lot."

She reached out and wrapped her fingers around mine. "I just had to come in here and say that before I leave."

Wait...what? "What do you mean, leave? Luke just got back into town." It pissed me off that I automatically jumped at defending Luke's best interests. I didn't want to care about him, but no matter how much I was hurt that feeling just never went away.

"I've already talked to Luke about this. He knows where I'm going, and he's very happy about it."

It was exceedingly nosey, but I couldn't help but ask, "Where are you going?"

Her smile brightened and it reached all the way to her beautiful green eyes. I noticed for the first time in my life that she had the same emerald eyes as Luke. It was unbelievable how much the two of them looked alike. How had I never noticed this? They had the same stark black hair, the same green eyes. They even had the same nose and cheekbones. When Ilene spoke again, I was positively floored. "I found an inpatient rehab facility in Houston. I leave tomorrow for three months."

The tears started running down my cheeks uncontrolled. "Oh my God," I whispered on a breath. I could only imagine how much this meant to Luke. I put a hand over my mouth and tried to stifle a sob. I wasn't sure why I was reacting as strongly as I was. I spent my entire childhood trying to be everything Luke needed since his parents weren't there for him. To see this woman finally stepping up to be the mother she needed to be... Well, it was too much. My heart swelled with pride for her.

"You gave me the strength to do this darling," she said with a sniffle as her own tears fell.

My chin jerked back in surprise. "Me? How?" In the past eight years, I hadn't said more than two words to Ilene. How I'd given her strength to do anything was beyond me.

"You don't know this, but I've been keeping an eye on you all these years. You are the bravest, most amazing person I've ever met."

Oh God.

"Your courage gave me the strength to do right by my son. I knew just by looking at you that the mother you were while that child was still in your belly was a hundred times the mother I'd ever been to my own child."

My heart absolutely broke when she said that. I was so moved by her declaration, but at the same time it made me feel raw to listen to someone talk about Ella. Even after all these years, it was still a pain that hadn't dulled.

"I know this might not matter to you, but I just have to say it. I love you, Emmy. For everything you ever did for Luke, everything you were for him, I love you, and I'm so damn proud of the woman you've become."

I stood and walked around the table to her side, and hugged her. We stayed wrapped around each other for so long I was sure everyone in the diner was staring. I just couldn't bring myself to care. After knowing this woman for so many years, we'd just reached a place that I never thought we'd get to, and that made me happier than I could have imagined. "You're wrong," I whispered in her ear. "That matters so damn much."

LUKE

I WOULD'VE RATHER HAD my nails ripped out with pliers and had salt dumped on the wounds than do what I was about to do. As I sat on her front porch, I had to work on my breathing to keep from hurling all over the Azalea bush in front of me. If I upchucked on Savannah's flowers, she'd have my ass.

I'd been sitting there for over an hour, waiting for her to get home from work, and the closer it got to the time she should arrive home, the more my anxiety twisted in my gut, making me nauseous. When her cherry red Lexus pulled up in the driveway, I wanted to take off running. I'd done two tours in Iraq, yet the idea of a confrontation with that blonde terror scared the ever-loving shit out of me.

When her eyes finally landed on my through her windshield I knew it was too late. She threw her car into park, opened the door and stepped out. Glaring daggers at me from over the roof, she crossed her and stomped up to me. "I'm so glad you're here, Luke." She said with an evil smile plastered on her face. "I just got me a new handgun, and I've been dying to break it in. You'll make an awesome moving target."

I ignored her barb and pushed forward with what I came to do. "We need to talk," was all I responded with.

"See, that's where you're wrong, *Deputy.*" Sarcasm dripped from her words as she hissed her reply. "We have nothing to talk about. You need to get your ass off my property before I shoot a few extra holes in it."

Rubbing at the tension building in the back of my neck, I held my ground resolutely. "Look, I know that you hate me and, honestly, now that I know the truth I don't blame you one damn bit, but I've got shit I need to tell you that might make you understand a few things. Is it too much to ask for you to hold off the fire power until we're done?"

She studied me for several long seconds, and I could see her fighting the desire to shoot my ass full of a few extra holes. There was a minuscule part somewhere deep, deep down inside of her, that people probably didn't know existed, that wanted to hear me out, and I was praying that part won.

Finally, she responded. "Fine. You've got exactly five minutes to tell your story." She turned and unlocked her front door, and right after it opened, she turned back to me before entering. "But if I don't like what I hear I demand the right to cut your balls off."

I had no doubt she meant that. She'd gladly rip my nuts off and keep them in a jar by her bed if she could get away with it. "Yeah... I'm not going agree to that, Savannah."

She shrugged her shoulders and pushed through her front door. "It was worth a shot." I was shocked as shit when the door didn't hit me in the face. She was actually letting me into her house. I glanced around to make sure there wasn't some sort of Luke Allen voodoo shrine in her living room before entering. "What, no altar or Luke doll with pins in the eyes? I'm a little disappointed."

She kicked her heels off by the stairs and removed her suit jacket. "I keep my shrine of torture in the guest room, don't worry."

"I'd expect nothing less," I deadpanned as I took in her house. There were pictures hanging on the walls and resting on the fireplace mantel. Some of her and Emmy, others with the whole gang. On the bookshelf next to the bay window facing the front yard, I noticed a couple pictures of her and Jeremy. I was surprised to see those, considering they hadn't been together for years. I didn't know the whole story behind their breakup, but it wasn't lost on me that there was still something between the two of them.

"You plan to stand there staring at pictures all evening, or are you going to tell me what you came here for? The clock's ticking." She tapped her watch to drive the point home.

I walked over to the recliner and took a seat across from where she was sitting on the couch. Her legs were curled up under her, all casual and confident. While I was on edge, Savannah was cool as a fucking cucumber. It was only after I leaned down and braced my elbows on my knees, that I made eye contact.

"A couple of months before I enlisted, my dad came to see me." I'd never wanted to tell this story to anyone, especially Savannah. But if I hoped for a chance of earning her forgiveness for what I'd done to Emmy I had no choice but to tell her the truth. As ugly as it was.

"He came back to town wanting money. My mom wasn't home when he showed up, and I thank Christ for that. I never wanted her to have to deal with that asshole again."

She shook her head in confusion. "I don't understand. I thought you never saw your dad again after he took off."

I rolled my neck, trying to loosen some of the knotted muscles. "I didn't want anyone to know. That's why I didn't say anything."

"Not even to Emmy?" she asked.

"Especially not to Emmy. I never thought I was good enough for that girl. She had this light inside of her, and I was this pathetic, damaged kid who clung on to her like a goddamn lifeline. She was the one good thing I had in my miserable life, and when my dad left, I was so fucking glad. Not because I wouldn't have to put up with his shit anymore, but because maybe with him gone, I'd finally have a chance at being good enough for her."

I found the courage to look at Savannah after my declaration. She was examining me with what I could only guess was a combination of pity and sorrow. I didn't come here to make her feel sorry for me, so I had to push forward. "I gave him everything I had. I wanted him to get the hell out and never come back, so I didn't even blink. I just wrote him a check for every dime I had in the bank and handed it over. I hoped it was enough to keep him from showing back up, but it wasn't."

"He came back?" she asked in a hushed voice.

"Yeah. A few weeks later, he came back, drunk as shit, demanding more money. I didn't have anything left, and I no way in hell I was going to let him anywhere near my mother. He wouldn't leave. Just kept going on about what a worthless piece a shit I was and how he regretted letting my mom keep me."

I scrubbed my hand over my scruffy jaw as I recalled that night in glaring detail. "I just lost it. I beat the shit outta the miserable bastard right there in my mom's living room. She came home and found the two of us going at it and threatened to call the cops if he didn't get out of her house. Since he had warrants out, he didn't blink before he bailed again."

Savannah surprised the hell out of me by leaning forward and placing her hand on top of mine. "I'm so sorry, Luke."

Not wanting to see the sympathy in her eyes, I stared down at my shoes as I told her the rest.

"Mom ran upstairs to get the first aid kit for my hand, and I followed him out the door to make sure he left. The last thing he ever said to me was that I was just like him. A miserable, good-for-nothing piece of shit that would blacken everything I touched."

Admitting everything out loud left me raw and bleeding, but I needed to get Emmy back, and this was the only way I knew how. "At that moment, I knew he was right. I was never going to be good enough for her. I freaked out after that night with her. I kept picturing her broken down and miserable, just like my mom. I couldn't risk her losing that light because she settled for me. So I did the one thing I knew would push her away." I looked up and caught Savannah quickly swiping at her cheeks. "Jesus, are you crying?"

She let out a strangled laugh. "What? I can show emotion when it's warranted, jerk."

I let out a laugh of my own. "Woman, I didn't even know you had tear ducts."

With a roll of her eyes, she teased, "And there goes our Hallmark moment." Savannah sniffled through her smile and gently said, "Go on."

"Honest to God, I thought I was doing the right thing. I thought if I cut off all contact, Emmy would find a guy that actually deserved her. I thought she'd be happy. Lord knows she deserved it. If I could go back in time I would have done everything differently. And if I knew about the baby..." I raised my hand when she started to interrupt. "It's no one's fault but mine that I didn't know. I didn't give her the chance to tell me, and I'll regret that until the day I die. But I need you to know that I'd give my life to take away the pain she's gone through." I leaned forward so she could see how serious I was. "I'll do anything, Savannah. I'd walk through fire for her. I need you to help me get her back."

I was terrified that, even though I'd just spilled my guts, she would still kick me out the door. I wouldn't blame her if that were the case, but she was the only person who could help me get through to Emmy. I wasn't above admitting that.

"Well, damn," she huffed. "I really don't want to like you."

I threw my head back and let out a deep belly laugh, thankful that Savannah could make light of such a tense situation. "Does that mean you'll help me?"

She blew out a breath and looked at me with a smirk. "Yeah, I'll help. But I want something in return."

Uh oh.

"What's that?" I asked cautiously.

"You see, I've got these speeding tickets..."

CHAPTER TWENTY-NINE

EMERSON

IT HAD BEEN a few days since my talk with Ilene Allen and I was still reeling. What she said hit me so deeply it was the only thing I'd been able to think about. Our conversation, and thoughts of Ella ran through my head on a continuous loop. It took a great deal of concentration, but I managed to pull myself out of my head long enough to get my work done at the diner. I was in the middle of the lunch rush and wasn't paying attention when the bell over the front door of Virgie May's rang. When I turned to greet another customer, I was assaulted with the stench of cheap perfume. Allison was standing there in all her slutty glory. She had one hip cocked, her hands resting at the waistband of her barely-there skirt. The smug smile that was stretched cross her face wasn't really that intimidating, considering she had a busted lip and black and blue bruises, thanks to Savannah's ass kicking that no amount of caked on concealer could hide.

"Sorry, no dogs allowed in the diner." I grinned back at her then turned to help my customers.

"Bitch," she mumbled under her breath because she was too chicken shit to say it out loud. "I just wanted to let you know that I'm pressing charges against you and Savannah." She said with evil glee, like a cat who ate the canary. "I'm going to make sure you two pay for what you did to me."

I turned back to her with a roll of my eyes, and cocked my hip as well, mimicking her stance. "I'm not sure what you're talking about, Allison. What did Savannah and I do to you?" I asked with mock confusion.

"Oh, please. Don't give me that shit. You know exactly what I'm talking about."

I tilted my head to the side with a fake thoughtful expression, then I turned to all the customers sitting at their tables, staring at the exchange between me and Allison with blatant interest. "How many of you were at Colt's two nights ago?" I asked the entire diner. More than half the people raised their hands. "Do any of you recall the events of that night?"

Missy Clearwater spoke up then. "I don't recall you and Savannah doing anything, but I clearly remember Allison tripping and falling on her face." Missy looked in Allison's direction. "Sweetie, you really should rethink heels that high if you're planning on getting *that* drunk. It's just not wise."

Trying my hardest not to laugh, I wished I'd had my phone on me to capture the moment, because the look of disbelief on Allison's face was legendary. "Anyone else remember Allison falling on her drunk ass that night?" I asked.

Mr. Clements stood then. "I do remember seeing you and Savannah leaving Colt's the other night. Neither of you fine ladies even glanced in Allison's direction, so I'm not sure what she's talking about."

It was then that I remembered why I loved living in a small town so much. I might have lost my way for a little while, and been the subject of the gossip mill, but Savannah and I were loved by the people in this town, and when you have that kind of love, they'll take your back through thick and thin.

"Are you fucking kidding me?" Allison shrieked. "Y'all all know what those two bitches did to me. Just look at my face!"

"Now, there's no need for name-calling, Ms. Crabtree. If you can't be polite to our little Emmy here, then you just need to be on your way. This is a fine family establishment. You'll do well to remember that."

God, I loved Mr. Clements.

"Unbelievable!" Allison's shrill voice was really starting to give me a headache. "Well, Luke was there, and I know he'll back me up."

Right at that moment, as if he'd just been waiting for the perfect opportunity, Luke strolled through the doors of the diner with a determined look on his face. He was heading straight for me when he caught sight of Allison. She immediately grabbed on to his arm with a death grip and plastered a pathetic look on her face.

"Honey, you know what Savannah and Emerson did to me Thursday night! Everyone is claiming I slipped and fell, but I know the truth and I want to press charges." She batted her fake eyelashes at him, and I had to fight not to throw up in my mouth. "You'll help me, won't you, baby?"

Luke looked at me with a blank expression then glanced back at Allison. "Ms. Crabtree. You can't press charges against someone just because you got drunk and fell down in a bar. The law doesn't work that way."

"B-but..." she stuttered. "You know. You saw what they did to me."

Luke pulled his arm from her grasp and came to stand beside me. "I didn't see anything," he stated in a voice so cold it sent a shiver down my spine. "But I do know one thing, if you weren't such a conniving bitch, maybe the people in this town would back you up when you needed them."

Whoa. What now?

"Despite what these people saw or didn't see, I feel confident when I tell you that you got I'm sure what you deserved. Now you need to get the hell out of Emmy's diner." He stalked over to where Allison stood, and if his size wasn't enough to intimidate, what came out of his mouth next most certainly was. "And don't come back. If I ever see you near Emmy or Savannah again, I'll arrest you for harassment."

"This is bullshit!" Allison yelled.

When Luke got in her face, I was almost a little scared for her. "Woman, are you deaf or just plain stupid? Get. The. Hell. *Out*."

Allison spun on her heels and practically ran out the door. It wasn't until she was gone that Luke turned his attention back to me.

"You're about as welcome here as she is, Lucas," I told him in a monotone voice. Just the sight of him caused an ache behind my breastbone so acute it hurt to inhale.

"Luke," he replied.

I crossed my arms over my chest and glared at him. "Excuse me?"

"Luke. Not Lucas. You only call me Lucas when you're pissed at me."

He has a lot of fucking nerve.

"Well, seeing as I can't stand the sight of you, saying your full name is kind of fitting, don't you think?"

He leaned down, his face going soft and gentle. Damn it, but it was a really good look on him. When he reached up and tucked a strand of hair that had fallen from my ponytail behind my ear I couldn't suppress the tremble it caused. "I don't care if you can't stand the sight of me. I don't care if you hate me until the day you die. I'll always be your Luke."

All of the air seemed to have been sucked out of the room. I couldn't breathe when he looked at me like that. I didn't have any fight left in me. "Please leave," I whispered weakly. I didn't have any witty comebacks or mean, biting comments. I just needed him to leave for my own peace of mind.

He nodded his head and the heartbroken expression on his face stripped me raw. He walked out the door without turning around, and it took all of my strength not to run after him.

I SAT on the bright green grass and ran my fingers over the grave marker. I'd picked a pretty, shaded spot for my precious baby that's close to my parents and Grams so she'd never be alone.

"Hi, sweetie."

I'd occasionally come to the cemetery and just sit quietly at my daughter's grave. Other times, it gave me comfort to talk to her. I knew she wasn't there, that her spirit wasn't in the ground, but it gave me a sense of peace to pretend.

Today was one of the days I needed that peace.

"I don't know what I'm doing, honey. I'm so damn lost right now. Your Daddy really is a good guy." I traced the name in the grave marker over and over. *Ella Michelle Grace*. "If you were here, he'd be wrapped around your little finger. He would have been a great daddy."

I sat silent for several minutes. "I don't want to love him," I said in a hushed voice. "But I can't stop."

"No one said you had to," The unexpected voice gave me a start, and I jumped, spinning around on the seat of my pants to see Savannah standing behind me. "I thought I'd find you here," she said as she sat next to me. "Hey there, honey bunch," she said to my daughter, running her finger through the carving of her name.

After several quiet seconds, I turned back to my friend.

"What are you doing here, Savvy?"

She took a deep breath and met my eyes. "You're my best friend. I know you, and I know this stuff between you and Luke is really taking its toll on the both of you."

I looked at her curiously. "Both of us? How would you know it's taking a toll on him?"

The expression that crossed her face morphed to one of worry. "Okay, I'm going to tell you something, but you need to promise not to freak out on me. Deal?"

It was safe to say she was making me nervous. "What's going on, Savannah?"

She turned away before answering. "Luke came to see me yesterday."

I jerked back in shock. "What do you mean, he came to see you?"

"He came to my house. He wanted to tell me some things in the hopes that I'd change my opinion of him and maybe help change yours too."

I let out a humorless laugh. "The dude must a have death wish. He should know better than that." When she didn't respond, my head jerked around to find her worrying her bottom lip. "Savannah?"

"Ithinkyoushouldtalktohim." She spoke in such a rush that all of her words blended together.

"You what?"

"You promised not to freak out on me," she said as she held her hands up.

"I didn't promise shit. What the hell do you mean you think I should talk to him, Savannah? You're the one who's practically made it your life's mission to make him miserable. You *hate* Luke."

She pulled her hair into a ponytail at the nape of her neck before releasing it again. "I know I said I hated him... hell, I *did* hate him for what he did to you." She looked at me beseechingly. "But he told me some things that explain so much, Emmy. You owe it to yourself to hear what he has to say." She took both of my hands in hers. "This is killing you. You aren't being fair to yourself. I don't know anyone who deserves happiness as much as you do. You're the only one standing in the way, honey."

There was no way I could be mad at her when she spoke with so much heart. Savannah was typically sarcastic by nature, so when she spoke with so much emotion it tore at me.

"Traitor," I joked in an attempt to lighten the heavy mood.

"You know I'm always on your side." She leaned over and wrapped me in a hug, and we sat there for a while, just looking at my daughter's marker. "She'd have been so lucky to have the two of you as parents."

Savannah saying that made me laugh and cry at the same time. "Luke and I might drive each other insane, but I don't doubt for a second that Ella would have had more love than any child could handle."

Savannah grinned and kissed my temple. "The two of you would have driven her freaking crazy. She would have had to run to her Auntie Savvy on a regular basis just to escape being hugged to death." My heart felt lighter just listening to Savannah talk about Luke and me as parents.

She was right. If Ella were around, I had no doubt Luke and I would drive her crazy trying to hug and kiss on her all the time.

"You going to talk to him?" Savannah asked as we stood and started back toward our cars.

I bumped my shoulder into hers and smiled at the best friend a girl could ever ask for. "I'll think about it."

CHAPTER THIRTY

LUKE

TREVOR LOOKED at me with a combination of concern and humor. "You sure you want do this, man? He was really fucking pissed the last time you saw him."

I grabbed my keys and started for the front door. "Hell no, I don't want to do this."

Trevor threw his hands up in the air. "Then why are you?"

He didn't understand the complexity of the situation. If I had any chance at all of reclaiming the life I'd had in Cloverleaf eight years ago, I had to make things right with *everyone*. I already won Savannah over, so that meant I just had one person left.

"It's just something I have to do, Trev."

"I might've been able to patch up the occasional bullet wound during battle, but I can't work fucking miracles, Luke. You come back here busted to hell, I'm just gonna have to take your ass to the hospital."

I gave Trevor a slap on the back and opened the front door. "That's a risk I have to take, brother. Wish me luck."

I was out the door and heading down the stairs when he hollered down "You won't need luck. You'll need a goddamned body bag."

I HIT the lights on the cruiser and bleeped the siren. The pickup in front of me slowly pulled over to the shoulder of the road and put on its hazards.

Here goes nothing.

I sucked in a deep breath and made my way to the truck. "License and insurance," I said, following procedure as closely as I could, considering this wasn't a routine traffic stop.

"You've got to be shitting me," Brett replied, pissed off beyond belief. "What the fuck am I being pulled over for?"

"Step out of the car, please," I said in a tone that made it clear it wasn't a request.

"Is this some kind of joke?" Brett threw his truck into park and opened the door to step out. "You want to tell me why you're pulling me over, *Deputy*?" He was clenching and unclenching his fists by his side like he was just itching to take a swing, my uniform be damned. It wouldn't take much for me to push him over the edge.

"I think you and I need to talk," I answered, crossing my arms over my chest to look as intimidating as possible. I didn't want to fight with Brett but I had to be prepared for anything.

He mimicked my stance as we faced off in one fucked up staring contest. "You planning on us having some *Lifetime* movie moment or something? Because I have to tell you, I'm really not in the mood to go all chick with you."

My desire to bust his lip all over again was quickly outweighing my desire to make things right. But I had to keep my shit together.

"Look, I get that you don't like me, and that's fine. I don't blame you for feeling like you do, but you need to know that I'm not going anywhere. What I did was fucked up. I was an asshole to each and every one of you, and I'm sorry. I shouldn't have bailed the way I did. I'm trying to make shit right, and that includes apologizing to you."

I had to take a deep breath to keep my thoughts straight. "I'd give anything to go back eight years and change what I did. I just wanted to tell you, face-to-face, that I'm going to do everything in my power to get Emmy to forgive me. That woman means more to me than my own life, but I also wanted to tell you that I'd like to make it up to you as well."

Deep breath... I can do this.

I lifted my arms to my sides and looked at Brett. "So do what you have to do, man."

He looked at me like I'd grown a third eye. "What are you saying? You want me to hit you?"

"Take a shot. I'm giving you a free pass. I won't duck or hit back. If this is what it takes for you to accept me back in this town and in Emmy's life, then go ahead. Take a swing."

Brett glanced from side to side like he was expecting someone to jump out and shoot him with a taser at any moment. "Have you lost your mind, Luke? I'm not going to hit a cop. You're in uniform for Christ's sake!"

"This isn't a set up," I declared as I dropped my arms back to my sides. "I'm out of ideas. I don't know how to get you to believe that I'm serious about this shit."

Brett ran both hands through his hair and started pacing back and forth in front of me. "You realize this is twisted, right? I'm not going to just wail on you so you can prove a point."

"Christ," I bit out in frustration. "Then what do I have to do, Brett? I'm trying to prove myself to you, and I don't have a fucking clue how to do that."

He placed his hands on his hips and hung his head as he let out a breath. "Well..." he started, then paused. "I have to respect you for putting it out there like that, even if it's all kinds of stupid." A smirk spread across his lips. "You serious about this? You'd really let me kick your ass just so you could get my stamp of approval for Emmy?"

It was my turn to laugh. "Not just for that." At the risk of sounding like a chick, I pushed forward. "You were my best friend before I left. I bailed on you too, brother. I want to get Emmy back more than anything, but I'd like it if you and I could be cool again."

"There's the *Lifetime* moment I was talking about," he exclaimed as he pointed at me and laughed.

"Laugh it up, asshole." I felt like a thousand-pound weight had been lifted off my chest. In all the time I'd been back, Brett and I hadn't been able to say more than three words to each other without one of us exploding. This could only be described as progress.

I reached my hand out to Brett. "We cool?"

He looked down at my hand skeptically, and the lightness I'd just been feeling started pressing down again. Maybe I'd misjudged the situation. Taking in the anxiousness on my face, he let out another laugh and shook my hand. "Yeah, brother, we're cool." He pulled me to him and gave me a slap on the back. "But I'm just gonna say this once. You pull that shit again, and I'll hunt your ass down and end you."

"Deal. I'll even give it to you in writing."

"Then I think we're good."

Thank fucking Christ.

After handing Brett's license and insurance card to him, he took off and I went back to finish my shift. When I walked through the apartment door, Trevor was kicked back in the recliner watching a game on my TV. "Well there's no blood, so that's a good sign."

"Do you work at all?" I asked, kicking his foot as I walked

toward the kitchen.

Trevor got up and followed me. I tossed him a beer and leaned my hip against the counter. "It's funny you mention that," he said after taking a pull of his beer.

"Why's that funny?"

"I've been scoping out locations to open up a tattoo parlor. I just made an offer on one today."

I'd known Trevor had skills when it came to ink. Hell, he was the one that did mine. He'd never really talked about it, so had no clue he was interested in starting up a business in Cloverleaf. "That's awesome, man. Where will you be setting up shop?"

He took another pull off his drink. "Well, fingers crossed, it'll be that building off Main about three blocks from Virgie May's."

I thought back to what building was there. He couldn't possibly be talking about what I thought he was talking about. "You're kidding, right? The old insurance company? That building's a bigger piece of shit than this one," I said as I waved my hand around the apartment we were standing in.

He walked over to me and gave me a slap on the shoulder. "Sure is, pal. Better be prepared for some manual labor if everything goes according to plan."

And with that, he walked out of the kitchen.

CHAPTER THIRTY-ONE

EMERSON

"IS THIS A SPECIAL OCCASION OR SOMETHING?" I asked my friends. It wasn't uncommon for them to come into the diner, but to have each and every one of them there at the same time, at the same table, was pretty rare considering they all had jobs and it was midday on a Tuesday. My gut told me something was up.

"Don't know what you're talking about, Emmy," Lizzy said with a shit-eating grin. "Can't a few friends enjoy a meal together every once in a while?"

"No," I deadpanned. "You forget that I know all of you, and I can tell when you've been scheming, so you might as well spill it." I scanned the faces of each one of them. I knew it was pointless to try and crack Savannah, Brett or Jeremy. Lizzy and Stacia were too busy laughing. Gavin was staring down at the menu like it was the most interesting thing on the planet. That left one person—the weakest link in my group of friends. "If you ever want to eat here again, Trevor, you'll tell me what's going on."

"Oh come on!" he said as he slammed the menu down on the table. "That's not fair, you know I can't resist the food here. You went for the jugular on the first move. That's such bullshit!"

Lizzy reached over and rubbed his back. "Ah, leave him alone, Em, you know he's sensitive when it comes to his food."

"Damn straight," he mumbled under his breath, still sulking.

"Someone better tell me what the hell is going on or I'm—" I didn't get to finish my sentence before the bell over the door chimed. I turned and saw Luke walk in, determination clear as day on his face. He stalked straight over to me, grabbed my face and slammed his mouth against mine. His tongue teased the seam of my lips, and when I opened on a sharp inhale, he nipped my bottom lip before his tongue dove in and tangled with mine. It took a lot of strength, but I managed not to melt into him as he gave me one of the best kisses of my life. I somehow managed to keep my hands clenched at my sides, but it was so hard not to grab hold of his hair and lose myself completely.

When he pulled back, we were both breathing hard. "Kiss me back, Emmy," he demanded as he leaned in for another kiss.

"No," I whispered weakly against his lips. I knew that the longer he had me in his grip the more likely I was to cave. I had to end this somehow.

"Kiss. Me .Back." His teeth were clenched as he pushed each word out angrily.

"*No!*" I tried to jerk away from him but he held tight to my biceps and wouldn't let go. A quick glance at my friends' table showed me that they knew this exact scenario was going to occur, and they'd come for front row seats. "I hate you guys," I muttered to them.

"We're going talk right now whether you like it or not," Luke demanded as he dragged me to the front door of the diner.

Pulling my arm with all of my might wasn't enough to get him to let go, so I planted my feet and tried my best not to budge. "There's nothing to say, Luke. Let me go, and get out!"

I was looking around to see how public our little scene had

become, so I didn't notice him pulling his cuffs out of his back pocket. The clink of metal jerked my attention to my wrist. One of the bracelets was wrapped around my wrist, the other one around his. "Have you gone mental? Uncuff me right now!"

"Not until you talk to me."

I looked around frantically at the diners sitting at their tables. "Do y'all see this?" I asked, lifting the arm that was cuffed to Luke in the air. "He's gone off the reservation! Someone call the sheriff!" Everyone quickly looked away and concentrated on their tables, including my soon-to-be ex friends. "That's it!" I hollered. "Y'all are all banned from Virgie May's. Every damn one of you!"

Luke started dragging me to the door, and I noticed Savannah jumping up and putting on an apron. "Order up, Lenny!" she called out to my cook.

"You don't say order up, Savannah. I say order up."

"What the hell ever. Just get me some damn food to serve these people!" That was the last I heard before the door closed behind me and I was pulled through the parking lot. "Where are you taking me?" I asked as I jerked on the cuffs to test the resistance. I wasn't getting away.

"Get in," was all he said in return. Luke opened the door of his department SUV and pushed me into the back seat, not very gently I might add. He took the keys to the cuffs out of his pocket and unlocked me right before slamming the door shut.

"The back seat? Is that really necessary?"

He shifted himself into the driver's seat and started the engine up. "At least this way, I know you won't be able to run."

He shifted into drive and pulled out of the parking lot. I sat in the back with my arms crossed over my chest and stared out the window. I *refused* to talk to him while he was acting like an asshole.

I stayed that way for several minutes as he drove, completely silent and taking in the scenery... until I noticed where we were. I sat ramrod-straight in the back seat. "No Luke, take me back right now!"

He didn't listen to me. He just turned off the car and got out. When he opened the back door he blocked me in so I couldn't make a run for it, and pulled the cuffs out of his pocket to lock us back together once again.

My heart was pounding so hard it hurt, and a cold sweat had broken out across my skin. "I'm serious, I can't do this. You need to take me back." I could see it in his emerald gaze, my pleas were having an effect, but he held strong to his goal, whatever that was.

He took my face in both of his hands and looked into my eyes. The love I saw shining down at me made me to tear up. "I need you to trust me, Emmy. I know I don't have the right to ask that, but please, just trust me this one time, okay?"

I didn't understand what had come over me, but at that moment I knew to my bones that Luke wouldn't do anything to hurt me. Something inside of me knew I could trust him with whatever he was about to do. And what was more, I *wanted* to trust him. Unable to speak past the lump in my throat, I nodded my head as a few tears slipped down my cheek.

He took the hand that was cuffed to his and interlaced our fingers before he started walking. I didn't know how he knew where he was going, and I wasn't going to bother asking. I could walk the path with my eyes closed so I just stared at the ground and followed his lead.

We finally stopped on the little hill and Ella's grave marker came into my line of vision. "Why'd you bring me here?" I asked on a whisper.

With a finger beneath my chin, Luke lifted my face to his. He wiped away my tears with his free hand and studied my expression before speaking. "Because I wanted to make a promise to you in front of *our* daughter." I let out a strangled sob and fell into Luke's chest. He wrapped both arms around me and pressed his lips to the top of my head. "I promise to always be here when you need me," he stated vehemently. "I don't want to live in the past anymore, Emmy. I'm not the same stupid kid I was back then, and I will *never* hurt you like that again. I'm a man who knows what he wants and what he needs, and what I need is *you*. I promise that I'll never disappear on you again. I can't promise that I won't make you mad, because I'm a guy and it's in our genetic makeup to do stupid shit, but I will promise never to cause you any pain intentionally."

I looked up into Luke's beautiful emerald eyes as he continued. "When bad things happen, I promise that I'm going to be the one that you lean on, and I will do everything in my power to make it better. I promise that if you take me back, I'll wake up every day with the single goal of making you smile, because when you smile, everything is right in my world.

"My life isn't complete without you in it, and I want you to know that I will *always* love you. There has never been anyone else for me. I'm going to love you until the day I die, Emmy. I just hope it doesn't have to be from a distance."

"Luke—" He placed a finger over my lips to stop me.

"I'm not giving up, Emmy. You need to know that." A smirk slowly spread across his lips. "You should just spare yourself the trouble, and take me back now."

His grin was infectious, and I found myself smiling back at him. "And if I don't?" I asked as a challenge.

He ran his fingers through the length of my hair and looked at the sky as if were contemplating his response. "Let's just say, I've got a few things up my sleeve that have the potential of making you a very miserable person."

I threw my head back and laughed. "That doesn't make me want to give you a second chance, Luke."

"Oh, it will. The things I have in mind will break you down completely. I'm not above playing dirty."

I traced the outline of his jaw with my index finger, watching its motion as it scraped along the stubble. "Good to know," I murmured to him.

"So what do you say, baby girl. Can you forgive me?" He started running his lips up and down the sensitive part of my neck, between my ear and shoulder.

"Depends." My voice came out deep, filled with love and lust.

"On what?" he asked as he traced the shell of my ear. "Just name it."

I pulled away from him and lifted our hands in front of his face. "On whether or not you plan on uncuffing me anytime soon!" I punched him on his arm for good measure.

He looked at the cuffs curiously. "I don't know, baby girl. I can think of a few things involving these cuffs that we both might enjoy."

A shiver worked its way down my spine. I really liked where his mind was going. As though he could read me like a book, he knew exactly what I was thinking and leaned down to give me a kiss. "I'll love you forever, baby girl."

Grabbing hold of his hair tightly, I lifted up onto the balls of my feet to intensify the kiss. "I'll love you forever, too, Luke."

EPILOGUE
EMERSON

THREE MONTHS *later*

"OH GOD, baby, that's so good." My head collapsed back onto the pillow as Luke slowly moved up from between my thighs. I caught the cocky glint in his eyes as he hovered over me. "Proud of yourself?" I asked sarcastically.

"Mmm," he buried his face in my neck. "I love how ready you always are for me." He moved back to my lips and gave me a feverish kiss as he pushed his cock inside.

"*Ooohhhh*, Luke," I moaned before realizing something important. I put my hands on his shoulders to halt his movement. "Condom baby. You forgot a condom."

He kept up his relentless pace, in and out, in and out. God, it felt amazing. "Didn't forget, baby girl. I don't want anything between us from now on."

It was so hard to pull myself out of the lust-filled haze Luke was dragging me into, but what he was saying was insane.

"Are you crazy? You know I'm not on the pill, Luke."

He pushed in to the hilt and stopped thrusting. Staring

down at me with such seriousness it made my belly flip, he said, "I know, Emmy. I want this with you. I want to be here with you every day while you get bigger and bigger with my baby in your belly."

Pushing the shock to the back of my mind, I continued to argue, "First off, you can't just decide to knock me up without my consent. Secondly, referring to me as getting bigger and bigger makes me want to punch you in the face."

Yes, we were arguing in the middle of really great sex, but that was just the kind of relationship Luke and I had. Everything about it was passionate. We fought with passion, and we loved with passion. It had gotten to the point where our public displays of affection made our friends gag. But our public fights were pure entertainment for everyone around us. It was just how we were, and we were both cool with that.

"I'm not going to knock you up without your consent, Emmy. I fully intend on putting a ring on it first."

I slapped him in his shoulder as hard as I could. "You did *not* just quote Beyonce while you're still inside me! That better not have been a proposal. If that's how you ask me to marry you, I'm telling you right now, I'll say no."

"Woman, can we finish this conversation after we've *finished*? You're so much more agreeable after I've made you come a few times."

I almost smacked him again, but then he started moving his hips, powerful and fast, and I totally lost my train of thought.

A *LONG* WHILE LATER, Luke and I were laying in my bed trying to catch our breaths. I was resting my head on his chest and had one arm draped across his washboard abs. He was running one hand up and down my spine in a slow, leisurely pace while his other hand played with my left ring finger. "That wasn't the real proposal, you know," he said after several minutes of silence.

I smiled and pressed a kiss into his stomach. "Good. Because there's no way in hell I would have accepted. Informing me you're trying to knock me up and saying you're going to *put a ring on it* while you're nailing me doesn't exactly scream romance, Luke."

I felt his chest rise and fall with his laughter. "Trust me, when I propose for real, you're going to freak. I've got it all planned out. No way you'll turn me down."

I interlaced my fingers on his chest and rested my chin on top of them so I could look into those endless green eyes I loved so much. "You sound confident," I chided, every bone it my body relaxed and sated.

"Oh, baby girl. You have no idea." He lifted his head and placed a kiss on my lips before laying back against the pillow. "And it's coming soon, so you better be prepared."

I laughed at the beautiful man beneath me. "I consider myself warned, Deputy Allen."

"I want a family with you, Emmy," he said more seriously. My laughter stopped at the abrupt change in his tone. "I wasn't here for Ella, and I wish I'd been there for the good and the bad. I want you as my wife, and I want us to have a family."

My nose began to sting, but I was determined not to cry. "Okay," I finally whispered. There was nothing else to say. Everything he'd just told me he wanted was exactly what I wanted too. I wanted a wedding. I wanted to marry Luke and have his children. I couldn't picture a life without him in it. It might be fast for some people, but for Luke and me, it felt like the logical next step. It was a long time coming.

About a month into our "official" relationship, Luke decided it was time we lived together. So one day he showed up at my house with all of his stuff packed in boxes, and went about moving himself in. I didn't really have a problem with that seeing as I hated his crappy apartment. And staying the night with Luke while Trevor was in the next room wasn't exactly a turn on. Trevor didn't seem to mind the condition of the apartment so he'd been more than happy to take over the lease.

"Okay?" he asked, shocked that I agreed so easily.

"Yeah," I smiled. "I said okay. But you still have to propose properly, Lucas Allen!"

"You got it, Emerson Grace soon-to-be-Allen."

With that settled, we fell back into a companionable silence for a few more minutes.

"How's Savannah doing?" Luke asked a few minutes later.

I took a deep breath and held it for a few seconds before blowing out a frustrated breath. "She's okay, I guess. She still won't talk about it and pretends like everything's okay, but I know it's all an act. I hate seeing her like this."

About a month ago I hired a new waitress at the diner. No one expected Jeremy to ever move on from Savannah, but when he walked into the diner on Charlotte's first day, he spotted her immediately and there seemed to be an instant attraction. The two of them had been attached at the hip for the past three weeks. Savannah had been trying to act like it didn't bother her, but I caught her looking in their direction several times, and the expression on her face always broke my heart.

Luke started the hair thing again. He knew it soothed me when he ran his fingers along my scalp and through my hair. "I know, baby. I'm sure it'll all work out."

Shoving the sad thoughts away, I pushed off Luke and climbed out of bed. "Speaking of Savannah... If I don't get my ass in gear, I'm going be late, and you know she'll kill me if I make her late for a sale at Nordstrom's."

I quickly pulled on my clothes and started running a brush

through my mussed-up hair.

"You sure I can't talk you into staying?" Luke asked. I glanced over at him lying in my bed. Correction... *our* bed. His hands were behind his head, accentuating his sexy biceps. My eyes roamed over his pecs, past his chiseled abs, to where the sheet was covering his manhood. He really was mouthwatering.

But I had something else planned. I loved Luke, and because of that, there were things about him that I had to put up with. But there was one situation in particular that still required retaliation. I made my way back to the bed with a little extra sway in my hips. "Baby, I'd love to join you in bed all day," I pouted. "But Savannah will kill me if I don't show."

I watched him watch me as I placed my knee on the bed and straddled his waist. I leaned in for a kiss as he took my hands in his and laced our fingers together like he always did. It was exactly what I'd been counting on. I moved our joined hands above his head, and he was so consumed with the kiss that he didn't register the metal clinking against the brass frame of the headboard until it was too late.

I quickly pulled away and hopped off the bed. Luke looked at me with a confused expression, and I couldn't help but laugh as I saw all the pieces click together in his mind.

"Emmy, what do you think you're doing?" he asked as he jerked his hands against the cuffs that kept him attached to the bed.

"This'll teach you to cuff me to you." I walked into the bathroom and put a coat of gloss on my lips before grabbing my purse and slinging it over my shoulder.

"Emmy, you can't leave me cuffed to the bed while you go shopping. You'll be gone for hours!" The irritation painted on his face made my revenge that much sweeter.

Skipping over to him, I placed a quick kiss on his lips. "I'll try not to be too long, baby, but I can't make any promises. I love you."

I headed out the door, laughing hysterically as he yelled my name over and over, shouted every colorful curse word in my wake.

I was asking for trouble. His payback would be brutal, but I absolutely loved this. I couldn't wait to spend the rest of my life with Luke.

We were going to have so much fun.

THE END
keep reading for an excerpt from the next book in the Cloverleaf series, Rising from the Ashes

RISING FROM THE ASHES EXCERPT
SAVANNAH

PAST

"I DON'T UNDERSTAND. Things have been great between us."

I couldn't bring myself to look into Jeremy's chocolate brown eyes as I ripped both of our hearts to shreds. I was a complete coward, and I hated myself for what I was doing.

"Things have been strained for a while, Jeremy, you know that," I replied in a weak voice, the lie tasting bitter and wrong on my tongue.

How was I ever going to convince him that this was what I really wanted when I couldn't even convince myself?

"That's bullshit, and you know it, Savannah!"

I recoiled, his tone harsher and louder than I'd ever heard it before. The anger burning in his eyes took me completely by surprise. Jeremy wasn't an angry person by nature. I'd never seen him the slightest bit violent in all the years that I'd known him. Hell, the man barely raised his voice a day in his life. Seeing him react with so much emotion was a brutal hit to my already shaky resolve.

"Jer," I whispered, "ever since Emmy—"

He cut me off, slicing his hand through the air. "Don't." His voice, low and cold, caused goose bumps to spread over my arms. "Don't you use what happened to Emmy as a reason to end us. What happened to her was a goddamn tragedy, and my heart broke for her, but that's not us, Savvy. That wasn't our loss, so it shouldn't put a strain on our relationship."

That wasn't exactly true. Emmy losing her baby was definitely part of the reason I was ending my relationship with the guy I'd loved since I was fourteen years old. There was no way I could let him know just how badly I'd let things snowball out of control after watching my friend hit rock bottom. Jeremy would hate me until the day he died if he knew the truth.

That was why I had to end things.

It had been two months since I made the decision that ultimately destroyed everything I held dear, and looking at myself in the mirror was getting harder and harder with every passing day. I knew if Jeremy found out what I'd done, he would be as disgusted with me as I was with myself. That wasn't a risk I was willing to take.

Like I said before, I was a coward.

I made the decision to end things because I couldn't handle the guilt of what I'd done, and the longer I stayed in this relationship, the harder it was to keep my shameful secret from Jeremy. This was going to hurt him. I knew that because I was already dying inside. But he'd eventually get over it, and hopefully, we'd be able to be friends again. Breaking up with him was the only way I could keep him in my life without running the risk of him eventually finding out and hating me forever.

I honestly thought that I'd be able to get past what I had done. I knew it would be hard for a while, but I never expected it to effect me so strongly. Every day I woke up, the first thing I wished for was to go back and do everything differently. But that was why people say hindsight is twenty-twenty, wasn't it?

I sucked in a deep breath and tried to steel myself for what I had to do next. I was about to drive the final nail into the coffin that was our relationship. If I drug it out any longer it would become impossible for me to stick to my decision.

"I can't do this anymore, Jeremy. Watching what Emmy went through showed me how short life really is. It got me thinking that you're the only person I've ever been with." I squeezed my eyes shut tightly, swallowing past the lump forming in my throat. Hurting Jeremy was the last thing I ever wanted to do, but it was inevitable.

"We've been together since we were fourteen. I want to see what else is out there. I want to be able to date other guys. We shouldn't have to tie ourselves down to one person at nineteen, Jer. We're too damn young. There's too much that we haven't experienced yet. I just feel like we're holding each other back."

If the expression on his face could physically maim, I would have been dead on the floor.

"So, let me get this straight," he hissed out, his jaw ticking from the strain of trying to stay composed. "You're breaking up with me because you want to fuck other guys. Am I getting this right?"

"It's not like that." I hated how he'd basically broken down my carefully constructed reason. Deep down, I knew there was no other guy. There never would be. I didn't want anyone but Jeremy, but because of my actions, I couldn't allow myself to have him anymore.

"*Am I fucking right or not?*" he roared.

Tears instantly started streaming down my face, unchecked. What I was about to say would do irreparable damage. Worrying about keeping my tears at bay wasn't even a consideration.

"Yes," I whispered in a hoarse, broken voice.

One word.

One word was all it took for Jeremy to look at me like I was the scum of the earth.

One word, and I had crushed all hope at having the future I truly wanted.

One word was all it took for him to turn and walk away without looking back.

One word, and I'd lost the only person I ever loved.

Read more here

And be sure to check out the rest of the Cloverleaf series

MORE IN THE CLOVERLEAF SERIES

Picking up the Pieces

After having her heart broken by the only man she's ever loved, everything seemed to go downhill for Emerson Grace. It's taken years, but Emmy is finally starting to pick up the pieces of her broken life. Until the man who destroyed her heart returns, bringing with him the pain of the past.

Running from Emmy was the only way Lucas Allen knew he could protect her from the demons he carried with him. After spending one perfect night together, Luke took off, certain he couldn't possibly give Emmy everything she deserved. Eight long years later, he's returned Cloverleaf to try and make up for his mistakes. He can only hope it isn't too late.

Loving Luke has always been easy. It's forgiving him that seems impossible. Now it's up to Emmy to decide whether to give him a second chance, or let him go for good.

Rising from the Ashes

Savannah Morgan found true love at a very early age, but a decision that she would regret for the rest of her life was all it took for her to lose the only person who had ever mattered.

For seven years, Jeremy Matthews has accepted being "just friends" with the only woman he's ever loved. Tired of living without her, he relentlessly pursues Savannah, determined to make her see just how perfect they are for each other.

But when Savannah's past mistake is revealed, threatening the future she so desperately wants, the fate of their relationship lies in Jeremy's hands. Now, it's up to him. He can either let go of the love of his life, or choose to rise from the ashes of the past and claim their happiness.

Pushing the Boundaries

Lizzy has watched each of her friends find their happily-ever-afters and settle down, one by one. And while she couldn't be happier for them, she's starting to crave that kind of love for herself. But with one failed date after another, she's beginning to think she'll never find her Prince Charming inside the borders of Cloverleaf.

Ever since stepping foot in her small town, Trevor has been enamored with Lizzy. But despite their

MORE IN THE CLOVERLEAF SERIES

intense chemistry, the feisty little redhead friend-zoned him before he could even make his move.

After watching her date every loser in town, he's finally decided enough is enough. And thanks to a drunken weekend in Vegas, he finally has the one thing he's wanted for so long. His ring on Lizzy's finger.

But just because he caught her doesn't mean he'll get to keep her.

Now it's up to Trevor and Lizzy to decide if they'll let fear hold them back, or if what they have is worth pushing the boundaries of friendship, in the hopes of building something that's even better.

Worth the Wait

Cloverleaf was Mackenzie Webster's second chance. It was the place where she dreamed of starting over and creating a new life for her and her children. She had a carefully thought-out plan for what this new life would look like, and nowhere in it was there room for a relationship. But the one thing Kenzie never counted on was meeting Brett Halstead.

Brett was all about fun and friends. "Long term" wasn't a phrase that fit his lifestyle. That was, until Kenzie walked into town and turned his laid back world on its head. Now he wants serious. He wants long term. And he wants it with Kenzie and her kids.

But her past refuses to go away, threatening to tear the couple apart.

Praying that the damage hasn't already been done, Brett decides to take on the task of breaking through Kenzie's walls to show her that love doesn't always hurt. She's a challenge he's determined to win, because a life with Kenzie is worth the wait. And he'll do whatever it takes to prove that to her.

DISCOVER OTHER BOOKS BY JESSICA

SECOND HOPE SERIES
The Little Things
Tangled Up With You

ASHLAND SERIES
Dead to Rights

WHITECAP SERIES
Crossing the Line
My Perfect Enemy
Turn of the Tides

THE PEMBROOKE SERIES:
Sweet Sunshine
Coming Full Circle
A Broken Soul
Should Have Been Me

WHISKEY DOLLS SERIES
Bombshell
Knockout
Stunner
Seductress
Temptress
Vamp

HOPE VALLEY SERIES:

Out of My League

Come Back Home Again

The Best of Me

Wrong Side of the Tracks

Stay With Me

Out of the Darkness

The Second Time Around

Waiting for Forever

Love to Hate You

Playing for Keeps

When You Least Expect It

Never for Him

REDEMPTION SERIES

Bad Alibi

Crazy Beautiful

Bittersweet

Guilty Pleasure

Wallflower

Blurred Line

Slow Burn

Favorite Mistake

Sweet Spot

THE CLOVERLEAF SERIES

Picking up the Pieces

Rising from the Ashes

Pushing the Boundaries

Worth the Wait

THE COLORS NOVELS

Scattered Colors

Shrinking Violet

Love Hate Relationship

Wildflower

THE LOCKLAINE BOYS

Fire & Ice

Opposites Attract

Almost Perfect

CIVIL CORRUPTION SERIES

Corrupt

Defile

Consume

Ravage

GIRL TALK SERIES:

Seducing Lola

Tempting Sophia

Enticing Daphne

Charming Fiona

STANDALONE TITLES:

One Knight Stand

Chance Encounters

Nightmares from Within

DEADLY LOVE SERIES:

Destructive

Addictive

ABOUT THE AUTHOR

Born and raised around Houston, Jessica is a self proclaimed caffeine addict, connoisseur of inexpensive wine, and the worst driver in the state of Texas. In addition to being all of these things, she's first and foremost a wife and mom.

Growing up, she shared her mom and grandmother's love of reading. But where they leaned toward murder mysteries, Jessica was obsessed with all things romance.

When she's not nose deep in her next manuscript, you can usually find her with her kindle in hand.

Connect with Jessica now
www.authorjessicaprince.com
Jessica's Princesses Reader Group
Newsletter
Instagram
Facebook
TikTok

authorjessicaprince@gmail.com

Made in the USA
Monee, IL
27 December 2024